City o

An anthology of Birmingham stories

The city at night

Edited by

David Croser

Birmingham Writers' Group Press

City of Night © 2018

Birmingham Writers' Group

Introduction © David Croser

A Midwinter Night's Tale © Alex Brightsmith

BMAG © Richard Preston

Eyes of Artemis © Christopher P. Garghan

Nerves © Steffan Jones

Our Anniversary © Berni Sorga-Millwood

Star Gazer © J.S. Spicer

The City Pubs at Night © Alistair Matthews

The Mummers' Boy © Matt Joiner

The Only Living Boy from Tile Cross © David Croser

The Wards of New Venice © Nicholas Doran

Cover design © 2018 David Croser

Published in Great Britain in 2018 by

Birmingham Writers' Group Press
Birmingham, UK

Birmingham Writers Group

Who we are

Birmingham Writers' Group welcomes members from all
walks of life from across the West Midlands – we're a mixed
bunch, and we enjoy new perspectives. All we require is that
our members are regular writers – published or otherwise –
and that they treat each other with respect.

What we do

Many people think of writers as solitary hermits – but the core
goal of most writers is focused upon other people:
communicating with an audience, whoever that audience may
be.

Different people join the Writers' Group for different reasons,
but some themes are central: we're here to support each
other's literary efforts, and sympathise with writerly woes, and
we're also here to provide constructive critical advice on each
other's work.

Our meetings take a variety of different formats. Often,
members will read out their work for others to comment on –
but we also host instant writing exercises, competitions, and a
range of discussion evenings on particular themes.

What we write

We're open to all kinds of writing. Our current membership features a lot of prose-fiction writers with a smattering of poets for good measure (pun ill-advisedly intended), but we're also open to non-fiction writers too; we've mainly focused on writing short stories and novels, but we've also covered radio plays and screenplays.

We do ask that any material read out at our meetings should be suitable for a diverse audience. Furthermore, whilst our range of ability varies, we are not the best group for people who are still mastering the basics – there are other writing classes available that are better-equipped to provide instruction on particular topics.

When we meet

We generally meet twice monthly: see our programme on the group's website for details.

After the official meetings, some of our members retire to a nearby pub for a less formal chat, but this certainly isn't compulsory! We also arrange additional social evenings elsewhere in other venues.

If you're interested in attending our next meeting, please go to out website, which can be found at www.birminghamwriters.org Have a read of read our 'how to join' page first – new members are welcome at all meetings, but for some of them it's better to have read the submitted manuscripts to get the most out of the meeting

CONTENTS

Introduction

Introduction

Night doesn't fall in Birmingham. It rises from the city's heart, from the streets and alleys where the sun never gets more than a brief look-in and, like the mist from the canals, it creeps over the rooftops and spreads up over the tower blocks. It conceals and protects things fair and foul with the same indifferent mantle.

By British standards Birmingham is young, having only been granted its city status in 1889, but the city and the wider West Midlands have a history that goes deep and far into the past. Way back *Beormingahām* was little more than a collection of huts along the little river Rea. If you had 20 shillings (one pound...) spare in 1086 you could have bought the entire place. A remote and marginal area. The main centres of population, power and wealth in the middle lands of England lay along the Severn, the Trent and the Avon. Not on some upland plateau bordered by the densely wooded and sparsely populated Forest of Arden and the bleakness of Cannock Chase. Some of that sense of remoteness and marginality has always persisted as time progressed and the city grew and expanded to become the workshop of world and Empire. 'Made in Birmingham' became both a badge of manufacturing pride. Anything you wanted Birmingham could make it. But where to pin that badge? This adaptivity and creativity extended to writers who were born or lived or were influenced by it.

Let's whisper a few names: Samuel Johnson, Arthur Conan Doyle, Lois MacNeice, Washington Irving, WH Auden, Roi Kwabena, Benjamin Zephaniah, JRR Tolkien, David Edgar, John Wyndham, Barbara Cartland, David Lodge, Jim Crace, Jonathan Coe, Joel Lane, Judith Cutler, Catherine O'Flynn, Clare Morrall, Austin Clarke.

Best not whisper them too loudly. Might make other places a bit envious. Might make them see us and try and pin us down.

What these names tell you is the sheer richness and diversity of the imaginations this city has touched and influenced and bred. Yet its marginality, neither in the North nor the South; neither Scotland, Wales nor Ireland, but fed through and filtered by every race, every colour and creed, have created a unique identity. And an elusiveness and ambiguity, that can be both difficult and attractive. Birmingham does that. You try to grasp it, clutching at a Jasper Carrot or an Aston Villa, and it has you, drawing you in with a glimpse of something else, something unexpected and wonderful.

Worked for me. Let our collection of stories do the same for you.

David Croser

Autumn 2018

About the Stories

Night is a time of marginality. It is a time when the rhythms and activity of the work and play change, becoming softer, muted, more subtle, and glimpsed beneath streetlights, through the darkness. You will find darkness of the heart and wonder in the shadows cast. There are tales of love and tales of fear, tales of joy and tales of loss. These are tells which reflect the variety of the city, its elusiveness and marginality. In 'Nerves' we meet a highly obsessive/over thinking male who goes on a date with his perfect woman which progresses from a nervous start to an awkward and inconclusive but - not disagreeable - ending. In 'Our Anniversary' Jasmine and Danny continue to meet up for their anniversary years after their death. They explore the city and become quite daring, which leads them into a perilous situation. 'Star Gazer' contains a search for a missing person, PC Sam Lane learns there is more than one lost soul in the city at night, and hope can be found in the most unexpected places.

For 'The City Pubs at Night' the pubs in the following story are authentic, as you would discover if you were to visit them. 'However the narrator is somewhat unreliable....
The Only Living Boy from Tile Cross' confronts the comfort found in darkness, and how it can helps us face the deeper darkness within. Our anthology concludes with 'The Wards of New Venice', a story about a dark alternate history of Birmingham. You'll wish you never compared Birmingham to Venice again. A dog is killed in "Eyes of Artemis' in the middle of the night, leaving nothing but a withered skeleton behind. As bodies begin to pile up, a woman with extraordinary powers, a detective in way over his head, and every eye in the city will hunt for the murderer. 'BMAG' is Birmingham Museum & Art Gallery: a fascinating place in the day... but at night, it's downright riveting. 'The Mummers' Boy' channels 1990's Birmingham, but it probably wasn't as vicious as the city here – was it....?

A Midwinter's Night's Tale

Alex Brightsmith

By the time I reached Highbury my fury had burnt off into the chill of the night. I was numb – numb inside and out – but still drunk enough to think well of my plan. Despite my grand gesture, I still wasn't respectable enough for Roz? Fine. I'd go back to the pool and fish out the glittering studs and hoops I'd flung there so many months before.

I'd been drunk that night, too. Drunk on lager and drunk on love and drunk on the thin edge of desperation that comes from seeing love is slipping away. But that had been high summer, the sky softly blue, and I hadn't had to touch the water. Now the sky was black, the moon a fleeting presence behind ragged clouds, and the best defence that I can offer for my plan was that this time I was *really* drunk – drunk enough to have told Roz what I really thought of her neat brown bob, of the concealer that she painted over her tattoo even though it was already hidden by her blouse, of the contacts (I can't say friends) with whom I had been insufficiently decorous. Decorous! I could name a time or two she hadn't been that decorous herself, but it only hurt to dwell on those. I'd grabbed leggings and a heavy knit dress, rammed my feet into moccasins and … gone. My hands were cold before I realised that I had no pockets, no keys – but what did I need keys for? I wasn't going back. Anything else I could sort out once I knew where I *was* going. But first, Highbury pool.

I followed the curve of the road until I reached the little grove of cypresses planted by the Townswomen's Guild (except that the sign, if I remembered right, didn't say *planted*, couldn't imply that they'd got their precious hands dirty). One of them was dead, spectrally pale against the dense dark wall of evergreens. Good, I thought, as I climbed the bank beside it. Bloody Townswomen's Guild. Bloody social expectations. Bloody, *bloody* respectability. Tears threatened; I paused, took a long, ragged breath, and passed on more circumspectly into the park proper.

It wasn't hard to find the pool, even in the gloom. It was closer to the edge of the park than it had ever felt, and I was barely clear of the looming evergreens before I discovered another hitch in my half-baked co-called plan: there were people picnicking under the willow. My feet carried me on regardless as I tried to persuade myself that my eyes were only playing tricks, but the figures didn't fade away, they only grew more solid. I began to hear their laughter and chatter, even snatches of song, began to make out a dozen figures, lit by flickering candles, began to see that they were dressed in a riot of improbable summer colour, with a kind of romanticized yokel air. Oh god, role-players? Students?

I'll give myself a pass on that one; I could hardly have expected it. You *could* picnic under the willow. Theoretically it was the perfect romantic spot, if you picked where you sat with extreme caution and didn't mind sharing your food with the geese. Roz and I had – *had* had – our own spot, reached from the other side, hidden away amongst the shrubbery, cool in the hottest summer; most people settled on this side of the water, but far enough back to enjoy the view without facing the scummy reality of the duck-fouled water. There was even a bench ... but this party were giving the bench a wide berth. Maybe they didn't know the area well enough to be cautious. Maybe it was too dark to see what they were sitting in, or they were too drunk to care. Either way, they'd spread their midnight feast right under the bare hanging branches of the willow, and they hadn't, so far, woken up the ducks and geese enough to regret their decision.

I kept walking. I could hardly start groping in the water whilst they were there, but I wasn't ready to turn tail and walk meekly away. Where would I go if I did? Not back to Roz, not yet. But I was saved from having to think about that too soon by discovering, as my feet carried me remorselessly closer, that there were birds strutting and pecking amongst the strangers. Coots and moorhens; they'd been hard to see in the darkness, and I saw them now with unexpected bitterness. I'd always thought them a little touch of the wild, not like the fat feral ducks and geese. Not just the waterfowl; I'd thought of this whole place as an incursion of the wild, and the birds' docility amongst the partyers was an unwelcome reminder that I was still in the heart of the city, where nothing was truly wild. least of all the girl I had once thought so free.

But they didn't give me time to think about Roz. I meant to sweep past them and work out my next move on the long walk on towards Moseley, but when they saw me coming the group swayed, shifted, and absorbed me.

They hadn't stinted on their costumes, I had to give them that. The cup that someone pressed into my hand (urgh, the sticky, decayed smell of mead, and I put it down untasted) had the heft of real glass, and there were no plastic fairy wings or pinned together sheets. The fabrics were lustrous and draped with skill, and the way the students moved in them you couldn't picture them ever wearing jeans or suits. In less time than I could account for I was in the heart of the crowd, drowning under a wave of insistent questions – my name, my demesne, whether there was a meaning to the serpentine tattoo coiling my wrist. I had an uncomfortable feeling that I was an object of curiosity to them, but oddly enough no sense of threat, and I thought I might as well play along. Periwinkle, I told them (hell, having dippy hippy parents has to come in handy once in a millennium, but you can stick to Peri, thanks all the same, and stop sniggering). I couldn't remember what a demesne was, and glossed over it. The tattoo was easier to slip into their mad fantasy world, but I didn't get a chance to really develop that theme. They'd started to fire off more questions, starting from the premise that it was a long time since strangers had stumbled across their revels. I guess the three months since September evenings turned nasty could seem an age, to the very young. They wanted to know if I knew any of their absent friends – Edward, Wystan, one even asked if I knew his Dad, though admitting that he wasn't local.

Of course I didn't, and I could see I was beginning to bore them, the supercilious snots. I pushed back, turning the questioning on them, asking if their costumes were *supposed* (I think they missed the implied insult) to be Shakespearean, and at that they thawed again. Oh, I knew the boy William, did I? He was the local boy done good – they were so proud of him, you'd think they'd had a hand in his success. My patience began to fail me. I was eighteen again, fielding condescending compliments from a student who hadn't expected me to recognise Wilde. But there was a touch on my bare arm, drawing me away, and that's when I met Hazel.

She gave me her name like an honour bestowed, like a caress. I'd seen her in the group, bored and aloof, but now she was right there at my side, her fingers tracing the coils of ink across my arm, and I looked at her properly. She was worth looking at. She seemed as delicate as a flower, but dressed in that diaphanous wrap on so frosty a night she must have been as hard as teak. It didn't show in the delicate curve of her neck or the perfect moulding of chin, and when she raised her head and smiled … this was no porcelain perfection, it was too warm and real. She had a smile that seemed meant just for me, and it was amazing, radiant. I just wanted to bask in it, like the first apricity of spring, and I did, for a while.

I was telling her the story behind my tattoo, the one that had seemed to bore her as much as her friends barely five minutes before. I had all her attention now, and I couldn't tell myself that my telling of the tale had improved. I was faltering through it, almost stuttering in time to the flutter of my heart, when a sudden scream ripped the cosy haze from the night, suddenly moon-bright and frost-burnt and sober.

It was a girl by the water's edge. She'd dipped her hand in the water, the idiot (I mean, who would do that in summer, much less in December – angry, drunk, heartbroken lesbians notwithstanding), and pulled it back with a scream. She was babbling now. Something burned, she said, and for a moment I took her at her word, wondering what sort of utter scumbag would dump chemical waste in the pool, but as the party rushed to her aid a bit of common sense kicked in. There was no ice on the pool, but the water must have been close to freezing. She must have been burning with cold, and so sheltered in her childhood that she didn't understand the sensation.

Hazel had rushed to her side with the rest; I could hardly blame her for that. I found myself drifting back, afraid to intrude, and before I knew it I'd backed up to the bench, and found myself sitting down with a jolt. The world swayed. I must have passed out for a moment – a long moment – for the next thing I was aware of was sitting on the bench, clinging to it for balance, the night empty and still around me.

I thought I heard laughter, carried on the biting wind, but I wouldn't swear to that. They'd forgotten me in their concern for their friend, even Hazel – there was a blade in that thought, keener than the wind – and they'd carried her off. I should go myself. I told myself so several times. I should go home, apologise to Roz. But I didn't want to do that, and it wasn't just pride, and if Hazel had any part in that it was only that she'd shown me what I should have seen long since. I'd been holding on to ashes for months, but even the bright, blazing thought of Hazel didn't make that an easier thing to learn.

I must have sat there for hours, picking at the rusty flakes coming off the bench, but eventually I got up and walked the long walk through the park, and by the time I reached Kings Heath it was almost late enough to knock up a friend and beg a bed. And so I did, and life went on.

Life does go on; it's a bastard for that. By spring I was back in a flat of my own, and coaxed out with friends. That was easier than I'd ever have guessed. One of the many things I'd never noticed as I tried to be the polite little wife that Roz needed was that we were drifting further and further from our real friends. So there was no awkwardness now, no shared acquaintance. We went each our own way, to the relief of our – of my – friends, and I hardly thought of her at all, except when the radio or the newspapers thrust that promising young MP Rosalind Grainge in my face. Rosalind! She'd been happy with Roz, when we first met. She's Miss Grainge, these days, when she's interviewed for the rolling news. I wonder if it makes her squirm? I wonder if she even remembers the days when calling her Miss earnt you a ten minute lecture on the uses of Ms and Mx?

But I don't wonder much. And even in those days, when all my studs and rings were stiff and new, and I still sometimes got off the bus three stops too early, I didn't give much conscious thought to Roz. It was Hazel who haunted me.

I saw her a few times in my dreams (though I never quite worked out, then, when I sometimes saw her and when I never did), and once in a crowd at a festival. I can't remember where, I only remember someone had warned me the scanners were over-sensitive and I wasn't wearing a scrap of metal anywhere, but the barman rapped my change impatiently on the bar and I turned to take it, and for the sake of tuppence I lost her again.

Spring had turned to summer by the time Mel appeared in my life, and I must have been doing a good enough impression of a whole person by then, because my friends started nudging me towards her. I shouldn't have needed much nudging; that should have been a sign. Mel was everything I've ever looked for, and when we stepped out together there's no denying that we made a good match. Tall and sturdy, steady and earthy, and if I didn't feel so sturdy as I used to, if my steadiness was only a pose, it must have been a good one, because Mel didn't take so much nudging as I did. Not at first, anyway. We had some nice times, as the summer ripened, but Mel couldn't make all the running forever. I could see her starting to realise it, and I gave myself a good kick. Roz was gone, Hazel had never been. Mel was here and real and beautiful, and it was about time I did something to show her I could see it. So I pulled out all the stops, and I did the only thing I knew – I packed a picnic and took us to Highbury pool.

Yes it's obvious, looking back. I must have wanted it to go wrong, or else I'm a bigger idiot than I ever realised. But even so, it started well.

We didn't come up through the pinetum, but parked further up, and crossed the meadow that I'd crossed so often with Roz. The moon was already bright, but the sky was still blue and the evening still warm. We came to the rocky little stream, and Mel looked doubtful, but we helped one another across it and disappeared into the prickly undergrowth, leading one another by turns along the little beaten track that runs above the water, until we came to the grotto where the stream tinkles down into the pool, and spread our blanket and our candles to make a world of our own.

It should have been perfect. If I'd been afraid of anything it had been that Roz would haunt me there, in the space that had been our own, but Roz hadn't any hold on me, anymore. It was Hazel who came between us, even though I'd never seen her here, amongst the holly and the yew. I kept thinking of the party under the bare branches of the willow, kept thinking that I heard them there.

My attention was all on the wrong side of the pool, and Mel stood it longer than I had any right to expect, but when she put an arm around me and I stiffened in her embrace, hushing her and straining towards the willow, she'd had enough. She asked, with as much dignity as she could muster, if there was somewhere I'd rather be, someone I'd rather see, and I tried to reassure her but the words all came out wrong. How could it sound sincere, when it was so obviously untrue? Her dignity gave way to anger, and that carried her out of the grove, just about, but I could hear that she was sobbing messily by the time she reached the second stream.

And I sat in the dark and listened to her go. I wanted to tell her she was beautiful, that she was nobody's sympathy date, but she'd have other friends to tell her that, and they'd be easier to believe. Besides, she was right. I didn't want her, couldn't fake it, shouldn't have tried. When I finally picked my way through the holly the sky was clear and the stars were bright – or at least, as bright as they get so close to Town – and I was utterly alone. Even the distant laughter that I though I heard was, surely, only in my imagination.

And life goes on. Sian came round next day to collect the few things Mel had left in my flat, and she was more annoyed with herself than with me. Myself, I was more annoyed with me. Sian might have been nudging, but there was no reason I shouldn't have held my ground. I was trying to tell her so as I sorted out a pile of CDs when I was stopped in my tracks. Sian stooped over me, puzzled

"Queen?"

"I – I never noticed the sleeve before."

And we went on, but when Sian finally left I looked up the album, because the tiny figures on the cover had been dressed like Hazel and her friends. The cover art, I found, was a painting by Richard Dadd. Not 'my Dad'. Just 'Dadd'. But Richard Dadd died in 1886, and I must have misunderstood. They hadn't asked if I'd known him, but if I'd known his work, and even in the midst of mourning what might have been with Mel I found an odd reassurance in the thought that at least one of Hazel's friends hadn't been quite the massive dick I'd thought him.

So I picked up the pieces, which were easier to pick up than I deserved, and I swore off dating and the year rolled on. I must have held my resolution for nine whole months, though I can't say I lived like a nun, and then Jenna came along, and she'd slipped though my defences before I even learnt her name.

At the time I told myself it was because she was so little my type that she'd slipped past my guard. She was china-doll pretty, delicate as a flower, and dressed for preference in floating layers. I was enchanted, against all expectation, and by some miracle she seemed to think I was worth looking at twice myself. By the time I realised what was happening it was way, way too late to argue with my heart, and I did the only thing I could think of − I took her to Highbury pool, to see if we could lay some ghosts.

We came up through the pinetum again. I couldn't take this delicate flower through the holly brush, and anyway, that wasn't the ghost I wanted to lay. We went right down to the water's edge, but even in the dusk the scummy green water was too big a dose of reality, and the hungry goslings even more so. We retreated to the slight rise that overlooks the willow-draped idyll, where we could enjoy the view but still watch the stars come out as well. We did, and it was lovely. We ate and drank and chattered. We watched the stars, with all the time a staid distance between us, and I told myself that it was too public a place for anything more, but I couldn't lie to Jenna the way that I lied to myself.

We lay on the bank, side by side and very chaste, and she took my hand gently. I remember her voice in the darkness, soft and firm and tender.

"I wasn't going to say this tonight, but I think it's time. I was going to wait and see if this could work, if you could forget."

"Forget who?" I asked unconvincingly.

9

"I don't know, but you're in love with her, not me. She had ringlets, I guess."

I cursed myself, and not gently – I didn't think I'd been quite so transparent about the change she'd made to her hair – but I didn't answer. She didn't need an answer. She only sighed.

"It's been lovely, but let's give it up, eh? Whilst it still is?"

And at least that night I went home in company, with a sisterly hug to wish me goodnight.

We parted on such good terms that she sent no emissary to collect her few things from me. I collected them myself, returning them on neutral ground, with a civilised drink between us. Scratching for conversation I asked about the battered children's book I'd brought back for her.

"Puck of Pook's Hill? My dirty secret. Kipling seduced me before I knew better …"

And she told me about the children who could converse with the spirits of the land because they still ran barefoot, and somewhere in the evening we found that we could still be friends. And that was it. The night I gave up dating. I had work, I had friends. I joined – don't laugh – I joined my local Townswomen's Guild. Yes, I know – but they're not in the least what you'd think. They're a good laugh, actually. And they get their hands dirty. And I met Sandy.

I know what you're thinking, but I never even thought about her that way. I'd never really had a best mate before, always been one of a gang. It was great to have someone to hang out with, no complications, no hangovers. We'd stroll amongst the pre-Raphealites in the central gallery like promenaders taking the air with our friends – I'd been doing my homework; I knew who Edward was now, and all his friends. She introduced me to Auden, W H – the boy Wystan, who had disappointed his friends by moving away, and any last doubts about ever catching up with Hazel again withered away. And Sandy knew Birmingham like a sister.

Sandy was good at picnics. The first time she'd suggest Kings Heath Park, and since it was better than staring at the walls of my flat I'd agreed, but when we got there she'd led me past all the weekend sports-stars, all the happy, conventional families, into a maze of little paths that ran through the patch of scrubby woodland I'd always taken for no more than a hedge. It felt immense, somehow, a whole world for us, a world of dappled sunshine and tiny glades, laurel and hornbeam and ash. It was like stepping suddenly into the real world, the distant sounds of traffic and of the high-pitched arguments from the grassy park only echoes from a dystopian fantasy. We'd eaten on a forgotten bench, watching the butterflies that chased one another through the cool shadows, and when we were finished we'd slipped over the railings at the far back corner, skittered down a steep path amongst the ivy, and come out under the railway, giggling like children and wondering if any of the staid family parties would wonder where we had vanished to.

It was inevitable that she would take me, one day, to Highbury, that we would cross that familiar meadow and help one another across the pebbly stream and through the holly and yew to settle above the little waterfall that had always seemed to belong to Roz and me alone. I had a wry smile for that, nothing more, and when Sandy caught my expression and asked I told her about it with a light heart, amazed to find it didn't hurt at all.

I think she was surprised, too. She gave me a long look, and then she kissed me chastely on the forehead, and I was too stunned to react until she'd moved away, suddenly very busy with the picnic hamper.

There was no hangover of awkwardness from the moment. We talked about the holly and the yew and the wide spreading oak, because I'd done my homework about those, too. I might be a city girl, through and through, but the city can't insulate us from the warp and weft of the country – it's still a part of the whole, and the raw thrust of nature breaks through, here and there, even if you edge it with flagstones. The night grew deep. Sandy placed a candle securely in a jar on the brim of the little waterfall, and it made the little grotto a room, closing off the world around it, giving her enough light to take out a box.

"Tell me I'm out of line, but, I saw this, and I know you like fairies."

Did I? I thought of my flat through Sandy's eyes, all the small things I'd accumulated over the last few years, always thinking of Hazel, never seeing the theme. I took the box, knew the name, a place in the Piccadilly Arcade I'd never been brave enough to enter, a little silver and amber fairy on a slender silver wire.

She was utterly beautiful. I sat staring at her, caressing her with one suddenly-clumsy finger, but my face must have told the story. Sandy was by my side, our bare shoulders touching.

"You don't mind? It's alright?"

I croaked out a yes, and she sat back, not hesitating but considering. Her eyes flicked across my face, considering the line of gold stars down my left ear, the little bone hoop in my right tragus, and then her firm, gentle fingers were at my right lobe, easing out the plain steel stud. She was warm and soft and close and I couldn't understand how I'd never noticed before how much I needed her, and she took the fairy gently from me and slipped it into place. She sat back far enough to admire the effect, but she didn't protest when I drew her close again.

We packed up pretty quickly after that. Tree roots and holly are all very well when you're twenty and stupid and haven't got anything better, but we had a choice of beds waiting for us. The car park was empty, and she was back in my arms when she suddenly stiffened in annoyance.

"My hat! I left it."

I laughed in relief and bounced off across the meadow to fetch it before she could protest, never giving a thought to my silver earrings or my empty pockets. Hazel was waiting for me under the willow tree. She really did glow, I noticed with detachment.

She was beautiful. Jenna couldn't have held a candle to her, whatever I had thought at the time, and Sandy wasn't even in the race. But I didn't love Sandy for her beauty, not in the portrait gallery sense, and I could see Hazel's beauty quite coldly now, even when she turned on the radiance of her smile. It was like the beauty of a meadow in spring time, or perhaps more aptly of a snow leopard, and the cruelty that I'd once thought I'd glimpsed there was a facet of the beauty, not an incidental flaw that could be disregarded.

"You've learnt to find me. I knew you would."

But I hadn't. It was only in that moment that I saw it all, Dadd's fairy folk, Kipling's iron charms, and I stood there naked, with silver and gold and bone in my ears, and soft summer clothes without fastenings. I must have had some armour, though, because I squirmed to hear her patronising tone, and I understood more than she realised. I understood that I could be her clever pet until she tired of me. She didn't have to make the offer; we both knew what lay between us. Suddenly I was a little sorry for her, in all her beauty and in all her power, enough that when I stooped to pick up Sandy's fallen hat I did it carefully, and met Hazel's eye very deliberately to tell her

"No, I've learnt something more important than that."

Her face asked the question, but I didn't think she had it in her to understand.

"Goodbye Hazel."

And I shifted Sandy's hat in my hands to touch the pin badge on its brim, and walked back to the car holding the steel pin of it very carefully all the way.

B.M.A.G.

Richard Preston

Hello! Yes, you!

You're new, aren't you? You'd have to be, looking so shaken as you are. Nobody told you, did they? No, you needn't check the speakers, this isn't a trick; you really are having a conversation with the Birmingham Museum & Art Gallery itself. No, please don't ask me how or why... frankly, it'd be very difficult to explain, and in any case I'm not in the mood right now.

Sorry, I hadn't realised how shaken you were... I always have been a big ham. I suppose it's not every day when the building you're in starts talking to you...

That's it, get your breath back.

Yes, it's always on the stroke of midnight that I can talk. I always thought it'd be fun to try it on those boring fundraisers they have after I'm closed. You know "Thank you all for coming tonight, I hope you enjoy my exhibits", something like that to liven things up. I mean, I know those events are important to keep me going, but I always feel like I'm window dressing, that my paintings are now something to have a quick look over instead of properly appreciating them. Still, better not, I suppose.

Mind you, that does remind me of an attempted robbery back in the 90's where I had rather a lot of fun...

Oh yes, quite a lot of the staff know about my being able to talk. It's always disseminated quite carefully, especially with the curators and city council members who might want to know just why the museum with the greatest collection of pre-Raphaelite art in the world is sapient. Well, yes, I suppose it was a bit rude of me to introduce myself like I did... No, I did not yell! I just... spoke quite loudly. Yes, of course there's a difference.

Look, I just wanted to have a chat with you – nothing wrong with that is there?

As I was saying, everyone who knows is quite careful. When you had your interview to become my new... what do you call it now, "Night Security Personnel"? Anyway, didn't Catherine ask you about how you'd react in unusual circumstances? If you could deal with the unexpected in a calm and professional manner? Didn't you have to have a physical, to see if your heart could stand any sudden shocks? Yes, it all comes into place now, doesn't it? I mean, it's not like she could ask you "Oh, by the way, the museum usually starts talking around midnight, are you okay with that?"

Well, of course I know what's going on during the day; I just can't say anything during that time - talking hours are after midnight only. I do sometimes give my opinion on how I'd like things to be run; I've been going on and on about how the Edwardian Tearooms need to buck their ideas up. One week they had overstocked on cod, so the next day they started serving fish lasagne, and people could tell it was leftovers! I have to admit, I was quite ashamed... people used to love coming to the Tearooms! And I don't just mean old people, but families as well. So ashamed...

Oh, well, of course I'm interested in the rest of the rooms as well... For example, I was one of those who pushed for more local history on the top floor. I was a bit on the fence about having so much open space up there... well, as much as any building can be on the fence! That said, I think it's worked out quite well. I really didn't like the idea of that gauzy thing by the stairs, but I've gotten used to it. It's just nice to have something up there again, you know? At least it won't be taken by that smug lump, Think Tank.

Damn it, I promised myself I wouldn't even think about Think Tank, and there I go again! I know it's been almost twenty years since I had to give up all my science exhibits... but it still hurts, you know? "Oh, don't worry, we'll have something else for you up here! We need to focus more to increase foot traffic!" I loved having that dinosaur round here, and you know where they eventually put it? In a skip, in pieces! I didn't speak to the curators for a month when I heard about that. Think Tank gets so many wonderful things, but is it grateful?

Ah... I've really let the cat out of the bag, haven't I? Yes, it's not just me that can talk to people. Actually, we tend to talk to ourselves more often than not. Some of the clubs are quite interesting to chat with, although they can be very blunt – I think they're chucking the riffraff out around this time. I usually chat with The Gas Hall, just to see how they got on during the day. I gave up trying to have any kind of conversation with Aston Hall long ago. Always so morbid... just because its architect was as crazy as a loon, it thinks it has to follow suit! Now there's a place that would give you an actual fright for the fun of it! There's a reason it has to have its security people go around in pairs at night, and it's not just because it's a large place...

16

Then there's The Ikon Gallery, but frankly it's a waste of time bothering with that one. Half the time, I can't even follow a single sentence from that pretentious Gothic hovel! Always acting like it's so much better than all the other art galleries for miles around... Do you know what is hanging on the walls of The Ikon right now? Some tinfoil, attached with electrical tape! And it's proud of that! At least when I have modern art, I have stuff that's actually art! City Council Chambers is right next door, of course, but it's always as dull as dishwater, and stuck-up to boot. I don't seem to have much luck when it comes to neighbours...

... Sorry, I was just thinking about Central Lending. I haven't done that in quite a while. Yes, just opposite Chamberlain Square, where the fountain used to be. Did you go in there much while they were... while it was being closed down? No, that's alright... not many people did go in. They all crowded round after it closed, of course. I know they'd let it get rather run down near the end, but I'd gotten used to having Central Lending just... over there, you know?

I'm sorry; it's been a while since I've really talked about this. The thing you have to understand about us buildings is that we need people. Without visitors, or residents, or employees, we're just husks taking up space. Did you know that The National Trust actually lets some stately homes fall into disrepair, just to show what that sort of thing looks like. I honestly can't think of anything more cruel. The point is...

Sorry. The point is that being with Central Lending at that time was just so painful. People only came in during the last few months to see what books they could get for 10p each. Nobody cared, and then it took so long to tear everything down...

Oh God...

I don't want to be closed for refurbishments again. I know my electrics need replacing, I know that... but it's three and a half years. I know there'll be some people walking around, like you and the others, but it won't be the same. I... I just...

I'm sorry. I'm fine.

Honest.

...

Ah yes, "Star of Bethlehem" by Burne-Jones... largest watercolour in the world. Well, it was... some university in America has one that's a bit larger. I can't remember. It's one of those cities that nobody can spell. Cincinnati or Massachusetts, I don't know. I'm told it's of an empty building. Hardly seems worth the bother, if you ask me. At least mine has people in it, doing things. My art tells stories. It makes you think.

My word, 6 o'clock already?

Well, this was certainly quite an evening for us both, wasn't it? I imagine your shift is coming to a close soon − I can always tell, you know. Perks of being around so long, I suppose. I imagine you'll have a few issues to raise with your manager... Still, if you managed to put up with me tonight, I daresay you can deal with anything.

Eyes of Artemis

Christopher P. Garghan

A city of a million people teems with life; even as the people concrete the woodlands, and replace the trees with glass, so life adapts around it. Rodents thrive; the sky teems with scavenger birds ready to gorge themselves on the mountains of waste, weeds and vines burst through neglected corners of brick. The inhabitants of the city had tamed their once destructive river, capturing it in concrete culverts and diverting its waters for the much more manageable canal networks, but even here, life endured.

Rea felt all this life from her nest high above the city. A terracotta tower built to glorify God had grown neglected, and now trees burst forth from the accumulations of dirt and soil deposited over the years. The young saplings, carried in the droppings or feathers of pigeons, were now higher than any growing from the earth itself. Rea heard the heartbeats of a million flying, scuttling, and creeping creatures, felt the plants growing inch by painful inch as they strove for the sun, and she feared the millions of pathetic screams and squeaks as those lives were snatched away to service lives faster, bigger, or more cunning than they. All this was a vista Rea had lived

19

with for the entirety of her life.

But tonight, there was something different.

A life vanished without a gasp, a scream, or the sudden rush of adrenaline as the body tried desperately to preserve itself. It felt as though the vital energy of the pour soul had simply been leeched away in an instant. Rea frowned, brushed her wild hair from her face and shut her eyes. She let the images from a million pairs of eyes flood into her mind, building a picture of the city more complete than any online map. A fly had witnessed something, but the vision of a fly was useless to humans, too broken and distorted through its thousands of segments.

She shook her head, and tried to focus on the limits of her own vision, a birds-eye view over a concrete jungle, where a new predator stalked the familiar paths and passages. She trembled, and the heartbeats of three million rats quickened in sympathy. A flock of seagulls circling the tower watched as Rea hurried down the dilapidated steps.

She knew that the life had been taken somewhere in the south of the city, in the Irish Quarter, one of the new flats built from converted factories, maybe? No. Though the fly's vision was poor, the musty scents, the smell of old paper and threadbare carpets were too old, too ingrained to be in anywhere as new. One of the old terraced houses, then? Those rows of old houses which had survived waves of regeneration by pretending to be invisible.

The Irish Quarter had once been the beating heart of the city; in ancient times, its crossing-point across the river became a focal point, from here markets had arisen, communities grew, and it became the nexus for a new town. Eventually, geography, politics, and economics had built the town into a city, and the ancient heart was forgotten, abandoned. The river was buried beneath concrete, the markets closed, the industry left, and instead of the bustling core of an international city, the Irish Quarter lay neglected, dirty, and bristling with the nature that advanced when humanity retreated.

Rea walked past boarded-up factories, and warehouses until she found what she was looking for, a row of early twentieth-century houses with sagging roofs and peeling paint.

A scream rang out from an upstairs window in a house halfway down the road. Rea smiled and ran towards it, and the volley of shouting and arguments in a language she didn't recognise – Polish, maybe? Lithuanian? – and hammered on the front door. There was a brief flurry of heated incomprehensible words and the door opened a crack to reveal a shaven-headed man of vaguely Slavic appearance with an ashen expression.

"What's happened?" She asked. Experience had taught her that people were used to the dance of salutations and small talk, when it didn't happen people tended to just answer the question – shocked that the niceties of human interaction had been sidelined.

Well, most of the time.

"Nothing. Go away."

The door began to close, but Rea put her foot squarely between it and the frame.

"The woman who just screamed, she found something dead, hasn't she? An animal? A dog perhaps?" She watched his face like a hawk, "But it isn't like anything you've ever seen. It's like it's been drained of life."

There was a hesitation, and the door was pulled back.

"What do you know of this?" There was a note of accusation in his voice.

"Nothing yet, I need to have a look at the body." She pushed her way into the dismal little house and marched upstairs, where a slight girl somewhere in her mid-teens stood with her hands clamped over her mouth, shaking her head slowly. She barely registered Rea, who swept past her and into the cramped bedroom beyond. Amongst a library of yellowing books and piles of paper lay something which could have once been called a dog. It was skeleton-thin, skin wrapped around the bones like old paper, discoloured, fraying, and crumbling away. Rea frowned and closed her eyes, listening and feeling for the masses of teeming lives, which *should* be just beneath the dead skin.

The world of the microscopic was one that she tried to avoid, the senses of the creatures which lived there were so basic as to be utterly alien. When she was younger, she had been fascinated by the multitudes which made up her own body, and naively assumed that she could 'watch' her evening meal work its way through her system. Instead she found herself overwhelmed by base urges, sudden jolts of instinct and chemical reactions and instead of experiencing her meal go down, the carpet experienced it coming back up. Since then, she kept her experience of the microscopic as remote as possible.

As she delved deeper and reached for those strange sensations, she found... nothing.

"What has happened? Who are you? Why are you here?" Rea's investigation was interrupted by the trembling voice of the girl in the hall. Rea shook her head and turned to concentrate on the girl, trying to re-adjust her senses to the familiar human ones.

"I'm here to find out what happened to..." She started, and gestured at the mummified dog on the carpet.

"Lotinka..." The girl squeaked, "Her name is Lotinka. She belonged to Mister Puening."

"Mister Puening?" Rea asked, "can I speak to him?"

The girl shook her head and shrugged.

At that moment, the man how had greeted her at the front door appeared at the top of the stairs, whispered something to the girl and walked into the room, arms crossed over his broad chest.

"What happened here?" He demanded, angry with himself for having been bamboozled by this strange woman poking around his house.

"This dog is dead." She began to explain.

"I can see that!"

"No, you don't understand. This dog is *dead*. Totally, completely. There should be an entire ecosystem still alive in her, gut bacteria breaking down her last meal, bacteria eating up her flesh, white blood cells still fighting to stop them. Lotinka has none of that. I've never found *anything* so lifeless."

"But how did it happen?" He grunted.

"I. Don't. Know." Rea grunted in response. "As I said, I've never seen anything like this before. I'd like to speak to Mister Puening, though. Perhaps he knows something."

"I don't know where he is." He admitted, "he came home earlier, locked himself in his room, and neither of us saw anything of him, until Kasia found his dog."

"He locked his room?" Rea asked, tilting her head on one side, "then how did the girl—how did Kasia find the dog?"

"He *always* locked his door." The man explained. "He must have left it open when he... left."

"Hmm." Rea grunted.

She turned her attention to the room, and the hundreds of books piled around the tiny space. There were titles in German, Russian, and half a dozen languages she couldn't even guess at. Even the English titles were bewildering scientific jargon. She flipped open a couple of books at random and the page-long equations written there were even less comprehensible than the titles themselves.

"Do you know what he was working on? And for who?"

"He paid rent on time, kept house tidy, never made much noise." The man shrugged. "I didn't ask."

"We have to find him; something tells me that Lotinka isn't going to be his last victim. I'm going to stay here and try to find some clue as to where he might be headed." Rea announced and began to sift through the piles of papers, handwritten notes, letters, and pages of results from some kind of experiments. Like the books themselves, Robert Puening's notes were a chaotic mix of languages, often switching between them half-way through a paragraph. Margins were packed with scrawled notes; arrows criss-crossed the page, and made references to other works. It was utterly indecipherable.

"Hello. What's this?" Attached to a long, rambling letter, there was a glossy passport photo of a bearded man in his mid-fifties. Green eyes stared through a pair of silvery spectacles glinting from the unkempt bed in the corner. "Is this him? Robert Puening? Good. That gives me something to work on."

Rea drew her legs up underneath herself and she shut her human eyes, opening her perception to the millions of eyes of her city. The gulls and pigeons of the skies scanned the streets from above, rats, dogs, and cats provided a street-level view, whilst the dizzying eyes of the insects filled in the gaps. So many faces! The struggle of keeping the panopticon in focus was draining, but Rea knew that it was the only way to survey a city so vast without a lead.

As the sun fell from the sky, the day eyes fell to sleep, to be replaced by the stark, ultra-sensitive eyes of the nocturnal hunters and prey. Several times, Kasia and her father moved to interrupt her apparent meditation, but her twitching, hyperalert state put them off, until the clock struck midnight and the Polish father decided enough was enough. He reached out to touch Rea's shoulder.

"It's no use." She said, stretching out from her position and trying to shake the feeling of being a million minds at once from her head. "If he's still in the city then he isn't showing himself. Oh and you should really close the blinds when you're inside. Anyone could be looking in."

With that, Rea folded a handful of potential leads, tucked them into her clothes, and made her way out into the night. The father watched her go, and then peered out of the window to see who might be looking in.

"Nothing but moths." He grunted.

As Rea walked past *The Orion Arms* pub, watching the way that moths danced in the streetlights to the fiddler's music streaming from inside the dusty establishment, she considered her next move. Was there even another move to make?

Had Lotinka been the final victim of Robert Puening?

Who could she turn to for help? The police would simply dismiss her as a loon, any friends she might claim to know had long since moved on – not that they would be any help – and there was nobody she knew even in passing who could make heads or tails of the bewildering books filling Puening's room.

Feeling lost and, for the first time in a long time, alone, Rea casually broke into one of the many empty warehouses dominating the edges of the city, found a sufficiently dry corner, and curled into a ball to sleep, allowing her unconscious mind to flit between the living creatures of the warehouse to guard her as she slumbered. It was a restless night, as though eyes beyond those of the animal kingdom were watching her.

Just after dawn, she was startled awake by the

scattering of the rats, mice, and roosting pigeons by the flashing lights and wailing sirens of a police car. The siren stopped, doors slammed, and Rea heard human voices on the other side of the old brick wall.

"Frankly Detective, I've never seen anything like this, nobody has."

"You say that it was reported by a drunk?"

"Yeah, he came into the yard to piss. Guess when he saw the body, that wasn't a problem anymore."

Body?

Rea was suddenly as alert as a cat, and tried to get a clear image of the activities from the life around them, but the lights, the sirens, and the people had scared off anything with half-useful eyes. Instead, she carefully leaned an old wooden pallet against the wall and climbed up to see through the broken glass.

Three uniformed police were stomping around the concrete yard, taking photographs, writing notes, and yammering into radios whilst a man in a suit and tie was led to something indistinct but familiar.

"Jesus." He exclaimed, squatting down beside the shape, "are we... sure this is a body?"

"Yes, sir." The constable explained. "There was more to him when we arrived."

Intrigued, Rea pulled herself up through a missing pane in the window, and squatted on the wall, trying to see what had attracted so much attention. At the constable's words, the detective flew into a frenzy.

"What do you mean 'there was more of him?' get a tent up around this body, immediately. You! Bring something to protect him from the wind." Without looking, he tossed his car key to the now suddenly mobile officers, and then pointed directly at Rea. "And you, this is an active crime scene. Unless there's something you want to contribute, I suggest you stop contaminating the evidence before I have you arrested for obstruction."

"I know who you're looking for, if that helps?" She shrugged, and clambered down from the wall. The detective looked at her with deep scepticism, but he pulled a flip-notebook from his pocket and tried to lead her away from the body, but she squatted beside it and reached out with her senses, trying to find any trace of life. When the detective moved to pull her away, she spoke again, "The man you're looking for is called Robert Puening. I don't know who or where he is or why he did this, but I know that he'll strike again."

"My name is Detective Inspector Frank Close," he said, "why don't you start by telling me your name?"

"That isn't important!" She protested, as though the D.I. had asked for her shoe size. "What's important is stopping Puening before he can strike again!"

"How do you know Mister Puening? How do you know that he's behind this?"

"Fine!" She snapped, "My name is Rea. I know that every cell in this man's body died at the same time, because I can't sense any of them. Puening's first victim was a dog at number twenty-four Sluice Street. I don't know how he did it. I can't see him anywhere in the city, which should be impossible. It should be impossible because I can see everything through the eyes of the animals of this city."

Rea stopped; Frank was looking at her in that way that was wearily familiar; a mixture of scepticism, frustration, and withering pity.

"Yes, *everything*." She blew out her cheeks, "all right, ask me to prove it."

"You see everything that animals see?" He said, a half-smile on his lips, "all right, I'll bite... prove it."

"Ask me something happening right now, that I couldn't possibly know."

"Fine. What is Jackie, my wife, currently doing?" He asked, confident that she wouldn't be able to guess – he hardly ever spoke about his marriage, trying to keep the barrier between home and work solid, especially given the arrangements of their relationship.

"Do you have a picture of her?" Frank opened his wallet and handed her a picture of a smiling Jackie, taken last year in Tenerife. Rea studied it for a moment, and then folded into a lotus position with her eyes closed. An uncomfortably long period of time elapsed, before her eyes snapped open. "She is currently lying in bed with another man. He is dark-skinned, has no hair, at least on his head..."

"Mikey, his name is Mikey." He said, colour draining out of his face. "How could you possibly know that? Neither of us have talked about our open relationship to anyone!"

"I told you, I can see..."

"...what the animals see, yes you've said, but how?"

"I don't know. It's something I've always been able to do."

All right, so let's say I believe that you are, what, Doctor Dolittle? Why can't you see this Mister Puening?"

"Two possibilities, either he has left the city..."

"What? Your magic power stops at the ring road?"

"I can see through them, but not clearly. I don't know enough about the places outside the city to fill in all the blanks." Rea explained, exasperated at being interrupted. "...either he has left the city, or he is invisible."

"…and you think the latter is more believable?" Frank closed his notebook and simply stared at her then held his hand up before she could interrupt. "All right, come with me. You can keep your... eyes... out for him, while I see what we can learn through Police records. I'll send another detective to investigate his house, see if we can come up with something."

"You want me to come to the police station?" Her voice suddenly rose half an octave, and she tensed up. "I don't like police stations. It's where they take me when I'm arrested for 'vagrancy.' Police arrested me for begging, even though I don't beg – I find my own food; police arrested me for 'rough sleeping', even though I was on a perfectly comfortable piece of ground; they arrested me for trespass, when I was only sleeping in a building that has been abandoned for a decade or more! I don't *like* police stations!"

"Listen," Frank said, trying to reassure her, "if you help me catch this guy, I'll make sure that my colleagues never bother you again. Deal?"

Rea looked at him with deep suspicion, debating whether to try outrunning the inspector and disappearing into the warren of passageways, tunnels, and vents which dominated this part of town. Her legs twitched, on the verge of flight, when she saw something like sincerity in his eyes. She bit her lip.

"All right. Deal."

As they walked away, a cloud of flies dropped to the ground.

A police station tends to be one of three things, to the vast majority it's just another building on the high street which they don't think about too often, except to check that they are *definitely* doing the speed limit as they drive past it, to the men and women who work there, it's just another office building, the place where lunches are ate at desks and the dull paperwork is filed.

Then there are the other people.

Rea tried to control her nerves as she followed a few steps behind Frank into the place she had been dragged to more times than she could count. To the right led to the overnight cells where she would be dumped alongside drunks, drug-abusers, and violent thugs. She shuddered as Frank swiped a pass to take her through the door on the left, into an office building which hadn't been redecorated since the early nineties, where the sound of clattering printers, ringing telephones, and the low hum of conversation replaced the more familiar shouting, swearing, and vomiting which characterised her usual visits. Frank led her into a meeting room off to the side and asked whether she needed anything.

"Water. Please." She said, quietly.

"All right, I'm going to run everything we know about Robert Puening through our systems, you... do whatever it is you do, and see if you can track him down."

Frank sighed as he closed the door, but, conscious that Rea might be watching him through a flea, or a fly or something, he tried to keep his expression neutral. He retreated to his desk began to delve into the public records. Arrest histories, medical records, social media accounts, mentions in the press, anywhere that he might have left a digital footprint.

Whilst the search programs were running, he also started to investigate some of the sciences that Rea had mentioned finding in books in his room. He immediately realised that he was in way over his head – the pages of equations on even the simplest primers resembled alien languages, and the 'explanations' might as well have been written in Klingon.

"Listen to this." He said to the first detective who happened to wander past his desk "'...vector multiplets interacting along co-dimensional adjoint fields transform holomorphically and symbiotically.' Just what the hell does that mean?"

Skimming across a handful of equally incomprehensible papers, he spotted a couple authored by a J. Picklow of the

University of Birmingham. A good a place as any to start. He picked up the phone and began dialling; soon he was connected to a number in the University's Theoretical Physics Department.

"Hello? Is this Doctor Jamie Picklow? I'm calling on behalf of West Midlands Police, and I wonder if you can help me?" He began to explain that a murder had taken place, and the suspect's room had been found packed with articles and books about a topic that left him utterly bewildered, "so perhaps you can help me by explaining what any of this means?"

"I'll try." She began, clearly trying to strip the information down to its barest bones. "There was a theory in physics until recently that every particle in our Standard Model of understanding, had a symmetrical partner, which would help to explain why particles have mass... Anyway, 'Hypersymmetry' is the theory that combines that theory with additional dimensions. Several physicists believe that, if we were to encounter an entirely separate dimension, every particle in *this* universe would have a twin in the other dimension. Because of this, if the particles could be constantly supplied energy from the original universe, they could pass over and occupy the same space as their partners."

"Could a person transfer their own particles across?" Frank asked, trying to wrap his head around the concept. Doctor Picklow laughed.

"Ohh, we had whack-jobs who thought they could, of course. Obsessives who thought that by moving their mass into another dimension, they could create the perfect stealth technology. Then, there were the *real* loonies who believed that the Government had already done just that. I still get letters every other week from a guy from Germany who—"

"Robert Puening?"

"Yeah, that's him, but—"

"Do you still have the letters he sent?"

31

"Inspector, I don't keep every letter I get, but I'm sure I have some of his correspondence somewhere."

"Can you please sort them out for me? I'll be over in the next half-hour." Frank put the phone down and practically ran to Rea's meeting room. "I think I have a lead on Puening. A scientist at Birmingham University has been receiving letters from him. I'm going to go over there now and get them."

"We don't have time." Rea protested. "Ask her to take the letters to the biology department and arrange them in front of the lab rats."

Frank looked at her as if she was mad for a moment, then shook his head and walked back to the phone, working out how to convince a senior lecturer in theoretical physics to display her mail to an audience of rodents.

"*...the energy transferred must be similar to the energy used by the particles before their transfer. Please forward corrections if these assumptions may be challenged.*'" Rea finished remotely reading Robert Puening's letters through the blurry vision of the lab animals, shook her head, and opened her own eyes. "It looks like he succeeded in transferring himself across to a parallel universe. He's killing animals—"

"—and people."

"...by transferring their energy across to sustain the transfer. So long as he remains over there, he can just keep killing and we can't stop him!"

Suddenly there was a scream from the front desk and the police station moved like a machine, office workers began to file out of the rear of the building, whilst constables struggled into their stab vests, ready to repel any intruder. They watched in horror as a young officer running through the door collapsed into a silently screaming heap of desiccated cells. Frank grabbed Rea and pulled her under the meeting room table as another officer crumbled before their eyes.

"Stay down!" Close hissed, "I'm going to draw him away."

Close took a breath, before stepping out into the office, ready to run.

"Robert Puening!" He declared, "we know what you've done! Splitting yourself across two universes, maintaining yourself through the energy of innocent people? Very clever. What pathetic, selfish reason could you have for these murders?"

Rea watched with mounting horror as a desk cactus crumbled into dust metres from the detective, who had started to back away towards the door. She scrunched her eyes tightly together and returned to the eyes of the lab rats, trying to piece together any way of stopping the monster in his tracks. She cursed her own ignorance as she read over dozens of pages of illegible scrawls and esoteric maths. Suddenly a single line jumped out at her, as though highlighted on the page:

"Only particles on the same dimensional plane may interact with one another without the sacrifice of the energy of one to maintain the other."

She looked up and a mad idea occurred to her, what was so special about Robert Puening? She expanded her mind, and reached out to the birds and beasts of the city, feeling them all touching her on a level she had never been able to explain and dived deeper, letting her mind struggle in the alien waters of the microscopic. Strange senses surged through her, impulses guided her, and from the multitutde, she found enough unfortunate microbial souls and drew their energies into herself. Whereas Robert Puening had achieved his transfer through the deaths of billions of parts of a single animal, Rea took a minute part of a billion creatures.

She opened her eyes.

Darkness, all around her was blackness deeper than any she had ever experienced, but swarming in the dark were the firefly-lights of living things, creating a glowing approximation of her world. She looked around, there! That collection of lights still backing away towards the door could

33

only be Frank Close, and to the left of him...

"Puening!"

Green eyes turned from the shape of Frank Close and stared, wide-eyed in astonishment at her. His fifty-year-old body was the only thing of colour in this alien environment.

"That's impossible!" He roared, "I dedicated *years* to discover how to do this. How could you accomplish it in a single night? I *knew* I was right to follow you from Sluice Street."

"You have to stop this." Rea insisted, walking towards him, "with every footstep, you're leaving a trail of death."

"Stop? This power has made me a god! It is my decision who lives and dies, with this power I can topple governments, bring armies to their knees, and decide the fate of every insignificant life on this pathetic planet!" He laughed, "who are you to challenge a god? Some dirty wastrel from the streets!"

"There is *no* insignificant life." Rea threatened.

Rea advanced on the bearded man as he began to back away from her, then changed his mind and ran at D.I. Close. He held his hands inches from his glowing shadow.

"Stop! Another step and he dies! Get down on your knees, girl, and worship me!" He growled, voice shaking. Rea stopped and felt her mouth go dry. Puening twitched his fingers. "Now!"

He grinned maniacally as Rea slowly lowered herself to her knees, eyes burning with fury. Puening dropped his hand, and stroked his beard, as though trying to decide what to do with the supine woman in front of him. Rea, meanwhile, considered just what the so-called 'god' actually was – a vast conglomeration of organisms working together in tandem. For all her life she had struggled to understand humans, their minds were too complicated for her to ride on. Until now, she hadn't realised that making up that complexity was a swarm of simplicity.

"Good girl. Since you have managed to do as I have, you're too dangerous to be allowed to return to our dimension alive, so I offer you a proposition: Go back to your world and die at my hand, or serve me, here. Which will it be?"

"You've left me with no option." She whispered as she shut her eyes and bowed her head in submission. Puening nodded, and strode imperiously towards her. "I—"

Robert Puening stopped and clutched at a sudden cramping in his guts, his skin turned white as the pain spread quickly and inexplicably throughout his body. When he opened his mouth to scream, there was nothing but a cloud of sandy dust. He dropped to his knees, scrabbling at his throat, eyes bulging as he tried to gulp down a breath into the collection of cells which made up his lungs, the collection of cells now reduced to an inert powder. Rea opened her eyes and rose to her feet, leaving him choking on the remnants of his lungs.

"You left me no choice." She muttered, and slipped back into the world.

Only D.I. Close remained in the office to watch a naked Rea appear out of thin air next to a pile of shredded grey-pink flesh. He stood there as though frozen, glanced at the heap of bleeding lung on the floor and the materialising nude woman beside it.

"What happened? What *is* that?" He gibbered.

"Robert Puening's lungs. I remembered that we're all made up of thousands of little lives. I can't make sense of a whole person, but I *can* reach out to single-cells. I just did to them what Puening did to Lotinka and the man in the yard."

Close looked as though he was trying to wrap his head around it. Shook his head, and walked over to the cleaners' cupboard.

"So, the short answer is that he won't be bothering us again?

35

"Well, the rest of him will turn up when the energy runs out, but no, he won't be able to kill anything again." Rea said, eventually, throwing her dirty smock over her head.

"We'll deal with that when it happens." He said, blankly, "we'll deal with... all of this... Jesus Christ, how am I supposed to deal with this?"

Rea shrugged.

"Robert Puening is dead. Nobody else knows how to transfer—"

"—apart from you."

"I killed far too many today. I'm never using this ability again." She shuddered, then squared her shoulders and marched up to Close. She held out a hand. "I haven't enjoyed working with you, detective, but I couldn't have stopped him without you, so... thank you."

"Wait! You can't leave! There'll be questions, paperwork!"

"That's why they pay you, detective." Rea said, "just remember your promise, and I'm sure we'll meet again."

"Thank you, Rea." He said, smiled, and took her hand. "Assuming I'm not out of a job for this, I'll see you around."

"No," Rea smiled, nodding to a fly circling a ceiling light, "*I'll* see *you.*"

Nerves

Steffan Jones

Ruadri waited patiently above the canal at Brindley Place, leaning over the railing. A forced patience - he had already walked a circuit around both first-floor entrances of the bar trying to work out the best way to make an entrance.

You don't want too many people to obstruct the girls' view of you, he thought. *Especially if they're generally wearing blazers and appear to be having a lively banter after a tough five-hour day selling house alarm systems to idiots.*

Ruadri looked over at a few smart casual guys, girls and mixed groups laughing together, basking in the late summer sun shining in through the balconies and wide-open doors and windows.

He homed in on one trio in particular, standing and holding their glasses, swaying back and forth on their heels a little, laughing. They fucking wore dark green chequered blazers with beige or pinstripe trousers. It probably wouldn't be too hard for a girl like *her* to fall for guys like *them* thought Ruadri.

Still he waited of course. He people watched. He tried to distract himself with his language app in between bursts of left and right swiping on tinder and checks of the girl's progress Whatsapp. Obviously, there were far more swipes to the right than the left. That was the same for everyone thought, right?

She wasn't responding fast enough so Ruadri crossed the little canal footbridge so he no longer had to worry about prying eyes and what they may have thought about this loner standing outside the Pitcher and Piano, constantly checking his phone.

He decided to walk into the International Convention Centre. Only the canal-side entrance though, and not for too long. Just long enough to get a feel of the place and what they actually did there. Ruadri had not been in this city for too long and he wasn't used to the sumptuousness of the general Brindley Place area. Ruadri had spent the bulk of his weekdays in a claustrophobic tech office in Nechells after all. For some reason, the people he had met so far didn't believe this when he told them this.

His pocket buzzed.

Yep, she was here. The excitement modulated through his trousers with the text and right up his leg to his crotch… Not that it had been *that* long. The jittery importance of this date was more around getting over or getting his own back on the last girl and the way she departed.

"Hey, here now xx" it read casually, lackadaisically, unperturbed.

"Whereabouts? Xx" He replied. Screaming it inside in his head though.

"On the main floor" it read. *What main floor?!* He thought.

"Is that the canal floor or the first floor? Xx" he texted,

crossing the footbridge in a bit of a hurry, back to the bars and restaurants.

Ruadri pounded up the stone steps before remembering to contain himself with some dignity. He then turned left around the wall and back into the crowds of drinkers and smokers basking in the late summer sun, enjoying each other's company, having a great time. He stepped cautiously into Pitcher's. All the doors and windows were jarred open to let in more light.

And there she was. Tarah, well fit in her red dress with her neck length blond hair in a practical bun. She stood with a powerful posture neither in the centre of the room, nor exactly at the bar, but the room seemed to centre on her. The curves, and there were curves, appeared a little constricted against the dress but they were still just about the right size for him. She was neither slender nor large but there was just something about the way she held her confidence as she approached him that concerned and excited him all the same.

Ruadri stopped trying to piece all this together in as few microseconds as he had left before he had to open up his arms in some form of welcoming gesture.

"Hey, nice to meet you" he said with a smile while she also seemed to open her arms, for some kind of embrace, beaming.

She was saying something back but he had to concentrate on not wrapping his left arm around her waist not too tightly and land a disarming kiss on her cheek but not too heavily.

"How are you, how was work?" he asked. *Is this a strange thing to ask somebody first thing on a first date?* Ruadri's work was important to him and from what Tarah had said it seemed to be important to her too.

"Yeah good thanks" said Tarah. "I know I look a bit glammed up but it comes with the job you know, got to encourage the ladies".

"Err – yeah. What kind of customers did you have today?" asked Ruadri.

"Well some of them didn't know what they were looking for so guided them on that. I didn't get to actually sit down and assist with applying any makeup or anything today it was more like girls just browsing. I guess I was showing my newer staff how to get others to come over and take a look," said Tarah.

Her pitch was measured and in control.

"Oh I didn't think… I dunno. I guess I just had this image of you sitting down and getting your customers to just try everything on," said Rhodri trying to maintain a lively warmth in his voice.

"To be fair, most customers already *know* if they want to buy something or not and if they're just looking I manage to work that out soon enough too," she said.

Ruadri fought an urge to shake his head as he sensed some contradiction in what she had just said. He continued to smile back at her, still excited at the bubble of power and joy in front of him.

"Shall we get a drink?" he asked, trying to re-exert some kind of direction to the situation.

"Of course, that would be a fab idea" she replied, smirking.

Ruadri grinned to himself as he walked up to buff barman in a tight black t-shirt, towelling down the inside of a pint glass.

Ruadri didn't know if he was grinning because he thought he was feeling vibes that she liked him or just because he had come across a new kind of energy in someone he had not felt for a long time. She was different. He was trying to register a time in his brain when another date had made him feel this intimidated.

"I forgot to ask, what's your policy on the guy buying the girl a drink?" he asked Tarah.

"Are you a feminist?" she asked.

Ruadri looked into her big blue eyes and stammered a bit under the intensity of the question, clearly designed to trip him.

"I am - well the thing is - I'm definitely a feminist. I mean I - erm"

He paused. He thought on his feet.

"Well put it this way. I believe that the world would be a better place if more women were in charge."

He'd said the main thrust of what he meant to say and she blinked and smiled with those large, surely fake, eyelashes.

It seemed that she believed and accepted his answer and he was glad because this genuinely was the truth even if he felt nervous.

"Oh good."

Tarah laughed to herself briefly.

"You know one time a guy I dated once after a night out actually said he wasn't a feminist and I simply got up and walked out of the bar," she said, smiling wickedly.

Ruadri flinched and then quickly composed his face.

"Really, who would even say that?" he asked.

"I know right, it's like – awww - you don't think women should have equal rights? Aww that's soo cute, I don't think you should have sex..."

Tarah giggled to herself,.

41

Ruadri laughed along and nodded, feeling worried.

Was she talking to me then - or him? How could she remember something like that and say it the exact same way she might have said it to him?

Ruadri leaned up against the bar putting his elbows on the table top and wrapped his hand around the other relaxed, unclenched fist.

"What can I get you mate?" asked the enviably handsome barman.

Ruadri hesitated a little, as he had to think about what to order.

"Erm - what did you say was your favourite drink again?" Ruadri asked Tarah.

"Well I like cocktails of course" she replied.

"I'm mostly a wine man you know. Red wine, usually Malbec or Shiraz," he grinned.

"Oh. Oh okay. No, you did say that before I think. I can drink wine too. I mean I like it on certain occasions," said Tarah.

"Ok great" he smiled. "Back to the feminist thing, do we go half and half or take it in turns?"

"Well we take it in turns" she said,.

"Sounds good to me," said Ruadri, feeling a little smug again as if he'd won a £500 on a scratch card. He'd only ever managed to win £100 so far, but he only bought one, once a week.

"Excuse Me," said Ruadri as the barman had just about turned to disappear.

"Yes, boss?" he replied.

"What red wine do you have by the glass?" asked Ruadri.

"Erm - well all really, what do you want?" asked the barman leaning into his side of the bar and looking back up at the shelves.

"We have Merlot, Malbec, Shiraz, Rjoca".

"Oh Shiraz please, we'll have a glass of Shiraz" said Ruadri.

"So that's two glasses of Shiraz, yeah?" said the barman looking for clarification.

Ruadri smiled at Tarah quickly.

"Yes please".

The barman poured.

"I'm not usually that horrible you know, I just hate cocky wankers who can't respect women and still think they can get anyone," said Tarah.

"Oh right."

Is she looking for validation? *I'm so confused* he thought.

"No of course I mean I'd leave the table like that too if I were you" said Ruadri, recalling the scenario she had painted for him.

"You seem pretty fun to me," he added.

"Yeah exactly, I'm delightful," said Tarah again sort of giggling to herself.

Delightful... He thought to himself. *Yes, she does sound a bit posh really doesn't she. I love it!* thought Ruadri.

The drinks were poured.

"That would be eight, ninety-five then please, mate."

Ruadri pulled his wallet out There were too many loose coins clogging up the bottom. He pulled his card out and lightly slapped it on the machine. *That isn't too bad*, he thought to himself.

Ruadri began to turn away from the bar to pass Tarah her drink before something intruded his thoughts uninvited.

"Hold on wait a minute. Excuse me" called Ruadri.

The barman had just started serving another two guys next to where Ruadri had stood.

"Yes, mate?" said the barman quickly.

"How can it be eight, ninety-five? That doesn't make sense. I don't get it?" asked Ruadri. He immediately regretted asking such a question. He must have made a mistake but the barman was grinning. Ruadri shook his head.

"I'm sorry. Forget it," he fled back to Tarah. He studied her reaction. She simply frowned and then sort of giggled.

"Erm where shall we sit?" said Ruadri, wondering more to himself while looking about the room.

"Why don't we go outside on the balcony? It's still sunny you know," suggested Tarah.

Ruadri liked the idea. He loved balconies. He used to own one back in Southampton. Well he didn't own it. He rented, with his father's inheritance, before he lost it all. He spent a year doing an internship in life.

Out on the balcony things were still somehow going pretty great with this wonderful woman. When she called herself delightful earlier, she wasn't lying. Tarah was knocking back the wines at an equal but measured pace to his. In this sense Ruadri knew there was no way he could really tell how fast, much or quickly she would normally drink. After their first glass went down quite smoothly, Ruadri went back inside the bar. When he asked for two more large glasses of the same wine as before he noticed the barman was using the same bottle he poured from earlier.

"Wait, wait," said Ruadri feeling more confident.

The barman stopped and looked back up, looking a bit more pacified than when Ruadri first came in. Ruadri smiled and nodded to him.

"Yeah, okay. I guess we might as well take the rest of the bottle now".

Ruadri's smile widened. The barman who had felt so confrontational or smug before was now grinning back at Ruadri, almost in approval as if to say yeah *go get her son. Get in there.* The moment was brief. Now gone. It didn't matter what this hench barman thought. He had someone far more important to attend to. Ruadri sort of nodded his head impatiently now to the barman.

"Oh umm that will be ten, twenty, please," said the barman.

There wasn't really enough in that bottle to see them through to the end of the date, thought Ruadri. It was too late now though really. Asking for a full bottle really would make the two of them look like dangerous alcoholics. Ruadri slapped his card over the reader one last time and it beeped in response.

"Thank you" said Ruadri, giving the barman one last impatient smile before carrying the bottle and two glasses quite awkwardly really.

It was time to put on his charismatic façade once more as he stepped back out onto the balcony. The sun was more or less down now although the sky itself was still light. It must have been about 9pm. He was running out of 'last trains'

45

to get before he really did have to go, for there was no way a girl like this, exciting as she was, would allow a guy to stay over hers on a first date.

Or would she?

To be honest Ruadri quite agreed anyway, he wasn't 22 anymore after all, when he was first trying to master the craft of Tinder without falling in love. He would try to fuck this one on a second or third date at least. Then it would mean something less surreal and perhaps something could be built from that.

Tarah greeted him with an adoring smile when he pulled out the chair and sprawled his legs comfortably. She looked a little curled up in her seat, enjoying the twilight breeze. Her big, terrifyingly confident, blue eyes were now still big but with something different. Ruadri perceived an element of unexpected excitement or surprise in those big blue eyes.

"Nice to meet you again" he said, trying to be charming of funny. It probably came off as over dramatic and cheesy.

"Good morning" she said a giggle.

"So what were we talking about?" asked Ruadri, genuinely trying to remember himself. She had tipped him off balance again.

"Oh I dunno wasn't it politics or family or relationships and my sexual preferences or something?" suggested Tarah.

"Ah yes!" announced Ruadri, remembering. "Well tomorrow is a big day. I think Brexit's actually going to happen you know, it's disgusting but I've been following it for weeks". Ruadri looked over his shoulder at the Romanian trio sitting on the table behind them. A girl and two guys.

"Oh shit," he whispered tucking his neck into his

shoulders as if something was crushing him.

"Shhh, shut your mouth" she also whispered, lifting her eyebrows in light embarrassment. Ruadri took a seat in the chair with a strain far exceeding that justified by his age.

"Let me help you with that?" she said and half stood up to pour the bottle of wine. Her knees must have hit the top of the table and the wine still in his glass spilled over his lap.

"Oh my god. I'm so clumsy. I'm so sorry," said Tarah.

The way she said it made her sound somewhat mortified but her eyes told a different story. Ruadri could tell from her eyes she enjoyed the scene she had started to make. Ruadri could only smile and laugh along with her as he made for the serviettes that came out with the glasses from earlier. Then he stopped in the enjoyment of the situation to push his luck a little further.

"You will at least help me clean my lap though right?" he said with a smirk.

"Well usually I don't like to think that I *owe* anybody anything" Tarah said a little bit more seriously. "But on this occasion, I think you've earned it".

She did reach over, and their eyes connected for an electrifying microsecond. Then they both just laughed and got on with the actual honest task of drying his lap.

"I'll try to stay calm," said Ruadri grinning at her.

They'd more or less pushed the table a little further out in order to move their chairs closer to each other. She looked up at him again, searchingly.

"Oh god, don't start. I wonder what all the people around us must think we're doing," she said.

"It's alright."

He put his hand on her shoulder then ran his fingers down her waist gently but also in a gesture for her to sit up again. As she followed he pushed the part of her loose blond fringe, no longer in the work bun, out of her face. She sort of froze a little with anticipation or curiosity.

"I don't really care if they can see or not I just want you to notice something".

"What?" she asked.

"This".

He moved his fingers away from her strands of hair and splayed his hand over her cheek, holding it there as he leaned in to kiss. Her hand was still in his lap and he noticed her fingernails dig in to his thigh ever so lightly. She certainly returned his kiss and before long their lips were parting with equal enthusiasm and their tongues eloped. When they retracted back into their seats they just left both hands on each other's laps for a while in a genuinely comfortable silence. She made some kind of sigh.

"Whew. I wasn't expecting that you know," she said.

She pushed some more of her strands of fringe back into place somehow but her bright pink *benefit cosmetics* showcase lipstick had smudged over her lips in a way it probably wasn't supposed to.

"Oh I, sorry you...erm."

Ruadri placed his fingers over her lips, lifting his eyebrows but also grimacing slightly to indicate they needed to fix that. She laughed and pulled out a little pocket mirror thing.

"Oh god I'm such a mess," she said fixing it with something else from one of her pockets.

"Beautiful mess," he replied a little quieter, almost under his breath.

She smiled. It wasn't exactly clear what she thought of him saying that or whether it was a little too intense, but at least she didn't say "aww" or something like that.

"If you like messes you should see my room," said Tarah.

He looked at her hungrily. "Oh I mean, not now of course".

"No, no of course," he interjected, "I wouldn't dare to presume something like that on a first date."

After his trousers had started to properly dry they drank a little longer, talking about their plans, talking about their most recent partners and their 'rules' around dating. They joked, they laughed and Tarah's hand had not really left Ruadri's lap from earlier.

When he had finally made his way away from Brindley Place, passed the great, wheeled library and under a long underpass, night had pretty clearly fallen. Ruadri had to concentrate as he was still not yet familiar with this big city, well big for the UK but he also had to hurry.

By the time he was safely sitting on the train seat, he realised how exhausted he was from all the recent changes: The new job, the new city and a crazy new animal for a date. His eyes closed and he slumped in his seat. He could rest his eyes, as long as he still listened carefully for the station announcements.

"Gravelly Hill" said the feminine robotic voice on the train. Ruadri's heart jumped in that mini heart attack way you get when you haven't quite fallen asleep yet but think you are.

49

Our Anniversary

Berni Sorga-Millwood

The sun faded. Darkness crept across the sky casting elongated shadows on the windows of the Indoor Arena. Bony fingers protruded out of the middle of the water in the nearby canal, fracturing its reflective surface. Within seconds a withered hand emerged from the murky depth and inched its way slowly towards the bank.

Jasmine grabbed the concrete side and hauled herself out, rolling exhausted and unnoticed onto the walkway. It had been a long time since she last visited; each year was getting harder and harder. She panted and caught her breath and wondered how much longer she could keep going.

Up ahead, diners emerged sporadically from the Pizza Hut restaurant.

Tears welled up in her eyes as she recalled their last meal there together many years ago.

The clatter of high-heeled shoes on metal stairs distracted her from her sorrows. A group of girls, laughing and chatting excitedly, climbed up the spiral stairway and crossed over the canal towards the trendy bars.

Still shattered, she rested quietly as Friday night revellers milled past oblivious to her existence. A barge full of tourist returning from a canal trip pulled up and disembarked a few metres away. Amongst them was an elderly American couple.

"Well that was just amazing don't you think Jim?" the woman asked in a southern drawl. She brushed her hand down her floral skirt to straighten it. "A didn't think a small place like Birming-Ham could have so much canal."

"Well it wasn't as pretty as Venice," Jim replied, adjusting his American bald eagle cap. He sported a matching t-shirt with an American flag on it. Linking arms with his wife, he guided her towards Broad Street continuing their conversation.

"Not as nice as Venice!" Jasmine mocked, recovering her strength pushing herself up into a sitting position. Her satin, pink evening dress was heavily stained from silt in the canal. She pulled off and discarded old crisp packets and bits of rubbish and stood up cautiously, her legs were still a little shaky. She was infuriated by the couple's comments. "It's certainly way better than your Las Vegas or anything else you've got in America!" she shouted.

"And you could do with updating your wardrobe too. I mean, no one wears sandals with socks these days." She ran her fingers through her long, black matted hair and pulled out handfuls of twigs and leaves.

The doors of the Sea Life Centre nearby were flung open and people poured out. Families with small children guided toddlers and wheeled their buggies along the ramp. A young boy broke away from his mother's grip, ran towards Jasmine and stopped within a few metres. Jasmine glared at him.

"Look Nemo!" he said, stretching out a toy stick with an orange and white fish on the end and touching her nose.

"Stop that." She slapped it from her face. "You're not supposed to see me. Go back to your mother."

"You like Nemo?" the toddler asked. "I like Nemo. He my friend!"

"Get back here Sam, we're going to miss the bus," the mother called, rushing over grabbing his hand.

As she led him away he turned and pointed Nemo at Jasmine. "Why she wet Mommy?" But his mother couldn't see her.

"You're pull-ups are wet? You should have told me before we came out. Haven't got time to change them now or we'll miss the bus. You'll have to wait till we get home."

"Lady wet Mommy... lady wet!" Sam continued as he was strapped in his buggy and wheeled under the stairway towards the bus stop on Broad Street. A squelching noise behind her made Jasmine furious.

"Oh that's so typical of you to be late Danny," she turned pouting, as a man covered in gunge from head to toe slithered out the canal.

"Don't be like that darling. It's our anniversary."

He scraped mud off his face revealing pale, translucent skin and bony features.

"Look at you!" She eyed him disdainfully from head to toe.

"You could have made a bit more effort."

She continued berating him as he stood up and removed old newspapers and filth from his blue, threadbare suit. A large, brown stain was down the left side of his white shirt; he buttoned up his jacket to hide it.

"Sorry love," he grinned, flashing stained, yellow rotting teeth.

"I swear each year the amount of junk they dump down there is getting worse."

"Oh excuses, excuses!" She rolled her eyes.

"My right arm was stuck under an old settee some idiot chucked in, and my foot wedged in a shopping trolley."

He flexed and rubbed his arm.

"It's a wonder it didn't fall off." She flicked back her long black hair and smoothed it down her caramel neck.

"You look as gorgeous as ever. I love that pink dress, it accentuates your curvaceous figure," he charmed, meandering closer. "Your skin is as golden as autumn leaves. Time has been good to you."

He wrapped his arms around her waist.

She pretended to resist as he kissed her neck, but then her face softened and she embraced him resting her head on his shoulder.

"I miss you so much," she whimpered.

"Wish we could spend eternity together." He scooped her up in his arms and carried her through Brindley Place, zigzagging around tables and chairs outside Costa Coffee and past the fountain.

"That's a bit of an eye sore," she complained, as he sat her on a bench outside Birmingham Library. "Why are we stopping here?"

"Look across the road," he whispered.

The old register office was being demolished, but the sign was still clearly visible.

"That's where we were going to get married!" she gasped.

"Why are they tearing it down?"

"Probably to make room for another one of them funny shaped metal and glass buildings." He paused reminiscing. "You would have looked amazing in your pretty lemon dress. We were going to do so much with our lives and change the world." He sat down and draped an arm across her shoulder. "Then your dad and uncles found out about us and – "

"Stop! Stop it!" she screamed. "I don't want to think about it, not tonight.

If you'd picked me up on time like you promised it wouldn't have happened."

"It wasn't my fault. Things were different back then. Nowadays you see loads of all kinds of couples walking around holding hands and no one bats an eye lid."

"Are you deaf?" She glared at him, stood up and stormed off. He followed sheepishly behind.

She stopped, looked up at the library and shook her head. "All that metal stuff makes it look more like work in progress. What's wrong with good old bricks?"

"Mmm!" he tilted his head to the side to examine it. "It's different grant you, but I like it."

"You would," she snapped, and walked off towards a small child skipping along carrying a princess balloon. Jasmine approached her, tugged the string from her hand and snatched it away. When the little girl tried to protest, Jasmine cackled and shoved her rotting face towards her, which sent her running off screaming.

"Skeleton woman Mum!" she cried, throwing herself into her mother's arms. "Skeleton woman took my balloon!" The mother comforted the child and looked back, but all she saw was the helium balloon floating horizontally in the air.

"Stop being cruel, it's not her fault," Danny chided. He took the balloon from Jasmine and wrapped the string around a nearby bench. The mother walked up and untangled it. When she tried to give it back to her daughter she didn't want to touch it, insisting the skeleton woman was watching her.

Danny grabbed Jasmine's hand and pulled her away. They walked in silence past groups of volunteers dispensing hot meals and drinks to the homeless and less fortunate. In an office doorway, a man in a stained, beige trench coat sat humming to himself. As they passed him he clutched a half bottle of Lightening Cider tightly to his chest.

"Unholy abomination!" he shouted, hiding his face with the bottle. Passers-by thought he was mad and gave him a wide berth. "Dead is dead! You should stay in the ground like God intended!"

"Stop your ranting old man," Jasmine spat, marching back to confront him. "Who you calling an abomination you piece of trash?"

"Ahh, get away, get away!" he screamed, waving his hand shielding his face with the bottle.

"I might be dead, but I'm still a lot prettier than you will ever be."

"Leave him alone," Danny interjected pulling her away. "He's got enough trouble of his own." They walked back along Broad Street teeming with its usual Friday night revellers.

"Fancy a drink?" he asked, steering her across the road towards the clubs. Young women dressed in mini-skirts and balancing precariously on high heels, strolled past them. They shivered without coats or jackets, clutching their tiny handbags to their chest for warmth. Young men dressed in smart shirts and trousers with polished shoes, joked and talked on mobile phones. As Danny and Jasmine walked past the queuing crowd outside Bar Risa, they notice a group of men in Batman onesies and masks pretending to be super heroes entertaining the crowd.

"Pathetic!" Jasmine remarked. "They let in all sorts nowadays." She pulled the mask off one of them, tossed it across the road and giggled as he ran off to retrieve it looking perplexed.

"You're quite mischievous tonight," Danny said, escorting her to the front of the queue. "I like the new you."

"I'm going to party like it's 1989 again," she said excitedly, reaching out loosening a bouncer's dickie bow tie and dropping it on the ground.

They laughed as he hesitated and looked at it confused.

"Don't know how that came undone," he said, bending down to get it. "It's gonna be one of them weird nights again, Al."

Music pumped out from huge speakers on the walls as rainbow lights swirled overhead, washing the interior in psychedelic colours. The dance floor heaved with sweaty bodies, gyrating, twisting, twirling and twerking in every direction. Jasmine and Danny headed for the bar.

"Half these girls don't look old enough to be in here," he remarked.

"Careful, you're showing your age granddad." They sat on stools and looked at drunken people, wobbling and stumbling their way across the room. Several were slumped in corners. "Fancy mixing it up a bit tonight? It's a big anniversary."

"I'm gonna stick to my usual larger, and maybe a bit of cider."

"Well I'm deserved champagne. Can't stand those fancy Alcopops everyone's drinking nowadays." At the end of the bar were a group of people celebrating someone's birthday. "How about him?" She pointed at a blond haired man in a grey suit sipping a glass of champagne. "He looks a bit like you and I bet he's loaded.?"

Danny faked a yawn and tapped his lips with his hand. "Boring! Those city boys are lightweights and will be heading home in a taxi before midnight." Two women dressed in pink tutus approached them, started talking and were offered champagne.

"I think I might just do a bit of mixing up myself," Jasmine said, flicking back her hair. "Never been a blond before." She got up, brushed unnoticed past several people and stood behind one of the women. She took a deep breath, exhaled and then suddenly leapt onto the woman forcing herself into her body. The woman shivered and stumbled a little; one of the men grabbed her around the waist.

"Steady on love.' I think you need to sit down before you fall." He guided her towards a chair by a table in a corner. Jasmine shook her head, blinked and rolled her shoulders adjusting to her new body.

"Sorry, I don't know what came over me," she said staring up at the man. "I haven't had that much to drink; must be these new shoes."

"It's probably that flu tablet you took earlier," her friend said approaching with the others. "Them shoes are nothing compared to your usual killer heals."

Jasmine giggled and drank another glass of champagne. She joined in the conversation occasionally to avoid giving herself away.

On the other side of the room, a man in leather trousers and jacket gave her the double thumbs up. It was Danny; she waved discretely acknowledging him. He was with a group laughing and downing pints of lager. Jasmine wanted to swap places with him because the people she was with were boring. All they talked about were financial bonuses and fancy cars, which she had no interest in. She was still only mildly tipsy after five glasses of champagne. When they got up to dance, she faked tiredness, slipped out of the woman's body and sauntered across the room.

In a booth at the back sat a young lady wearing pink Doctor Martin boots and a matching leather jacket. She was so drunk she could hardly keep her eyes open.

"Lightweight," Jasmine commented, plonking herself down on her lap and wriggling into her body.She shook her head, flexed her arms and stood up. "That's more like it."

She took a few tentative steps but was approached by a man in a leather jacket.

"Oh!" He looked surprise.

"I thought you were out for the count."

"I just needed a rest." She grabbed the glass of double whisky from his hand and drank it. "Same again please."

She handed him the empty glass and sat back down. He grinned, went off and got two more doubles and returned quickly.

"Back at the office they said you're a one drink wonder, but you're a lot more fun." After the third glass, he grabbed her, pulled her close and kissed her. She resisted at first and looked around for Danny, but he was lost somewhere in the crowd probably enjoying himself. She pulled the stranger towards her and kissed him back. After a few more drinks she began to feel light headed, so she got up and headed for the toilet unaware he was following her. As she walked in to one of the cubicles and was about to shut the door, he pushed his way in and locked it behind them.

"Get out!"

"Come on, you know you want me," he smiled, pulling her closer.

"The guys at the office told me you're easy once you've had a couple."

"I said get out!" She pushed him back, punched him in the face, kneed him between the legs and ran out the toilet. Danny was at the bar. "I can't explain right now, just get me a cab," she said leading him out.

He escorted her to the taxi rank and they got in a black cab. In the lady's jacket pockets, she rummaged around and found keys, money and a provisional driving license with an address in China Town. The taxi dropped them off and they let themselves into the flat. Jasmine sat on the settee and shuffled herself gently out of the lady's body, leaving her asleep in the living room. As they left the flat together and walked back through the centre of China Town, Danny sat down on some steps and eased himself out of the leather-clad man.

"You want to tell me what just happened back there?" he asked as they walked past Chung Ying Chinese restaurant.

"She was in trouble. He followed her into the toilet and tried to... you know... do stuff."

"I'm going to smash his face in," he snapped.

"I didn't tell you because I knew you'd react like this. I don't want you getting anyone else into trouble." He put an arm around her shoulder and they walked towards the closed and dilapidated Silver Blades Ice Rink.

"That's where we first met,' she smiled, looking up at it.

"It was a Friday night," he laughed. "You couldn't even stand on the blades. You were grabbing the sides and trying to walk around the rink while everyone else skated past you dancing to YMCA. When you fell I caught you."

"You were so kind. You helped me up then you slowly skated backwards, holding my hands and pulling me along till I got used to it and could skate a little on my own." She paused. "I loved Friday nights and counted down the days till I saw you again. It was the only place I was allowed out with my friends. Most of the time they just left me on my own and went off with their boyfriends."

She looked down at her feet reminiscing.

"I got there early that evening and waited outside at the back like you told me to. Everything was packed in my suitcase including my birth certificate and passport. I waited for hours, but you didn't come. When Sangita eventually found me and told me what they'd done to you, I lost it.

She pleaded with me to go back home, but I couldn't live with myself knowing what had happened. I left her there and ran down to the canal, by then everyone had gone.

I tried to find you and was going crazy, shaking and stumbling and couldn't think straight, hoping you might be sitting injured on the bank somewhere."

She paused and signed.

"Then I saw your wallet on the ground and the thick trail of blood leading towards the canal. It was too late; you were gone."

She shook her head.

"You were the love of my life, what else did I have to live for?"

Tears rolled down her face. He squeezed her hand gently.

"They were going to send me abroad to get married to some stranger I didn't even know. I ripped up my birth certificate and passport and threw them in the canal, and then I sat on the side and watched as they floated away. My head was throbbing, I vomited a couple of times then everything went dark. Can't even remember climbing in."

"I was delayed at work; the staff meeting ran over by almost an hour. When I left they were waiting for me in a white, delivery van parked on Corporation Street. As I tried to go past they grabbed me, bungled me into the back and covered my head with a bag so I couldn't see their faces."

"My family must have notice my stuff missing and my friends must have told them about you." They walked in silence along Rea Street past Digbeth Coach Station and along the High Street towards the Peugeot Car Dealership.

"See that black convertible," he pointed. "I was going to buy something like that to drive us up to Scotland in after we got married. They'd only just come out, and I put a deposit down on one with my bonus. It was going to be a surprise wedding present. You always said you wanted to drive through the countryside and feel the wind in you hair."

A group of inebriated young men walked past them.

"What's that smell?" one asked, sniffing the air near where Danny and Jasmine stood.

"Probably the vomit down the front of your shirt,' his friend replied.

He examined the bottom of his shoes. "Haven't stepped in anything. It's revolting can't you smell it?"

Danny and Jasmine hurried away.

"Come on mate." His friend grabbed him and pulled him along.

"You've already slowed us down. The band's starting any minute and we need to get there before the doors close."

They crossed over the road and headed towards the thirteenth century Old Crown Pub, with its black and white timber frame leaning slightly to the left defying gravity.

"He's in for a fun night," Jasmine said. "That's the oldest building in Birmingham, and it's full of discarnate spirits."

"A mate of mine was in there once chatting up this beautiful girl. She was wearing old-fashioned clothes and a shawl, so he thought she was just a student from one of them universities dressed up for Freshers' Week. When he got up to get himself another drink and asked if she wanted one, she shook her head, said goodbye and faded right in front of him."

Jasmine laughed. "I bet that sobered him up quickly."

"He was out of there in a shot and has never been back since."

"Neat trick! I'd love to be able to do that." They crossed the road and walked up Deritend High Street towards a pub. In the past it had been painted a multitude of colours, but was now just black with faded gold lettering. A rock band was playing a Guns and Roses song as they went in and the crowd sang along. Stale alcohol and the smell of e-cigarettes reminded them of pubs from the past. At the far end of the room, a group of young people dressed in black and purple sat round a table. Jasmine felt immediately drawn to them and their bottles of whisky and gin.

A girl with purple hair, matching lipstick, pale makeup and thick black eyeliner, looked up briefly sniffing the air as she approached. But before she could alert anyone, Jasmine pushed her chest backwards and forced her way into her body. She gasped and slumped to the side.

"You ok babe?" the boyfriend asked. He had a silver nose ring and two ten pence coin earrings in his earlobes.

"A little tired." She faked a yawn.

"The night's just started, this will keep you awake." He reached into the pocket of his tight, black denim jeans, fished out a tablet and dropped it discretely in her hand. Jasmine examined the smiley face on the tablet and looked over to Danny at the bar. When he shook his head disapprovingly, she popped it in her mouth out of spite and washed it down with a gulp of Jack Daniels.

"Give it about ten minutes," the boyfriend said. She waited but nothing happened. She wasn't familiar with popping pills, but had smoked a spliff or two in the past. The giggles and munchies she got from it were amazing and she hoping for something similar. After twenty minutes she still didn't even feel the slightest buzz.

"This is a waste of time," she muttered, pouring and drinking a glass of gin. "You got anything stronger?"

The boyfriend looked perplexed. "Perhaps that one was a dud. I know a guy who's got something special. Stay here." He got up and disappeared in the crowd.

"Take it easy," said a man dressed in blue denim with a red and white bandana round his head. He sat down next to her. "You're not use to that stuff."

"Oh, and you are I suppose?" she snapped at Danny.

"I'm just saying you don't know what sort of stuff is in it. They put in rat poison and all sorts of cleaning products to bulk it out."

"You're just trying to scare me. It's a big anniversary and I want to enjoy myself. Just push off and stop trying to control me."

"Hey mate, why you talking to my girl?" The boyfriend returned confronting him.

"Sorry mate didn't realise." Danny stood up, held up his hand and backed away. "Don't want any trouble."

63

The boyfriend began to square up to him, but Jasmine squeezed herself in between them.

"He said he was sorry," she said, stroking the boyfriends face and massaging his ear lobe. "He was just admiring my hair," she smiled. "Now where's my treat? I want to feel really good." She deliberately rubbed herself up against him to make Danny jealous and laughed as he stormed off.

"Let's go outside."

They went out the door, round the back and down the side into a dim lit alleyway. Jasmine was a little nervous but knew she could defend herself if he tried anything.

"So what's this surprise then?" she asked, kicking away an empty can and a broken bottle.

"Cameras are everywhere apart from down here."

He crouched behind a large, green bin and took a silver wrapper and a lighter from his pocket. "Ready for the trip of your life?" Jasmine nodded.

She was feeling a little woozy from the pill and drink, so she lowered herself carefully to the ground beside him. Resting her back against the bin, she closed her eyes to quell the dizziness and caught a whiff of something burning. Her limbs were heavy and tingly; she tried to move them but couldn't. A strange feeling crept over her, she felt herself floating upwards. *Stop! I don't want it!* She wanted to scream, but her mouth couldn't form words properly. A needle inserted into her arm caused her to flinch.

The pain was excruciating, her lips trembled and she wanted to cry out but couldn't make any sound.

Seconds, minutes or hours later, something brushed past her and the hairs on the back of her neck stood up. She opened her eyes and gasped, green boots and a pair of shadowy legs ran past. Where was the rest of the body? A rat scuttled across her lap, climbed up her shoulder then hopped into the bin in search of food. She shuddered and turned to look at the boyfriend. His lips were moving, but the words came out in colours, bouncing off the walls and whooshing and echoing through the alley like a rainstorm in a tunnel. She tried to focus on his face; that too was beginning to change. His skin turned yellow and wrinkly, then it slid slowly downwards, pulling the flesh and muscles from his face revealing large, black eye sockets. Unable to close her eyes, she looked up at the brick wall in front for comfort, and then screamed. Giant, black spiders with oversized pincers were scuttling down it towards her. She shuffled backwards and tried to kick them away.

"Bad trip! Bad trip!" The boyfriend's words splashed against the wall in a green, slimy liquid and oozed down it. "Take deep breath," the skull face in front of her instructed with maggots and worms crawling out its eye sockets.

She yelled, punched him in the chest, and then dragged herself along the ground to escape from him and the giant spiders crawling up her fishnet tights and skirt. Mustering all the strength she could, she jumped up frantically and brushed them off. But each time she knocked one off, it multiplied and came back. A rat gnawed at the nail on her right thumb. She smashed her hand hard against the wall to get rid of it, but it sunk its teeth into her bone and held on. Another leapt onto her shoulder and got tangled in her hair.

Just when she thought things couldn't get any worse, a black dog with a nose ring and a skeleton face kept barking and trying to attack her.

She grabbed a broken chair leg from the ground and jabbed at it. It ran off but came back a few minutes later with a bunch of other ferocious animals.

Brown, black and white bears stood on hind legs a few metres away rocking and clawing the air, wild boars with pointy tusks grunted and cats and dogs looked on and shook their heads. She spotted some blue, flashing lights from a van behind them and sensed they were getting ready to attack.

"Get back!" she screeched, thrusting and waving the chair leg at them. "Don't come any closer."

"Put it down," said a small, green poodle with big, gentle eyes.

"We're not going to hurt you."

It sauntered slowly towards her.

"But… but you're a dog! Dogs can't talk!"

"Just put it on the ground," a blue Rottweiler demanded edging closer. Two others stood behind it with long, black sticks in their paws. "We're here to help. No one's going to hurt you."

"Just stop! Stop messing with my head!" she screamed, shifting the chair leg from one hand to the other.

"You're just having a bad trip," someone shouted from the crowd.

As she looked up distracted, the others pounced on her tackling her to the ground. Jasmine screamed and tried to push them off, it was no use. She felt a sharp prick on her shoulder as they sedated her.

'I want Danny!" she cried hysterically.

"Is anyone here called Danny?" a policeman asked the crowd of onlookers. But no one knew who he was.

"Danny I'm sorry!" she wailed.

As the paramedics put her in the ambulance, she scanned faces in the crowd desperately searching for him. He wasn't amongst them. Panic set in when she thrashed around and realise she couldn't escape from the body she was in. The drugs she'd taken must have somehow altered her ability.

Faces in the crowd were full of curiosity and pity. She hated being stared at and longed to be invisible again. As she twisted violently attempting once more to escape, paramedics restrained her and strapped her down to prevent her from harming herself. She wept exhausted unable to fight any more as the ambulance door slammed shut; conscious she was trapped in a stranger's body.

Star Gazer

J. S. Spicer

A copper sun melted into the horizon. As Sam Lane brought the car to a halt outside Ridgemont Care Home the first faint bruises of evening were dappling the Birmingham skyline. Switching off the engine, she turned to the passenger seat.

"Ready?"

Harry Evans squirmed, thick fingers adjusting his uniform. "Hate the crazies!"

"For God's sake, Harry, don't use that word. The guy's not insane, just elderly and a bit confused."

He snorted irritably. "Whatever. I've met him before. Guy's off his nut."

Harry levered open the door and hauled his bulk out of the car. Sam quickly joined him. After two years working together on the force she'd (almost) got used to being dwarfed by Harry's six-foot-four frame. And to his less than politically correct social commentary.

"Maybe you should let me do the talking."

He didn't argue. Harry preferred catching bad guys to community stuff.

They were met by a middle-aged woman, Mrs Quince. She

smelt strongly of cigarettes and was chewing an already well-bitten fingernail.

"So, this Mr Cotton, how long has he been missing?"

Mrs Quince relinquished the nail to blow out a thoughtful breath; folded up rigid arms as she pondered. "Must be at least a couple of hours. We realised when he didn't show up for dinner."

Sam glanced at her watch. It was just after 8pm.

"Mrs Quince, is Mr Cotton considered a danger? Either to himself or others?"

"Oh, Ambrose is a sweet old fella," she told them, arms unravelling to jolt nervously by her side. "Wouldn't hurt a fly. But he's vulnerable, you see. Lives in his own little world, so, he doesn't see danger. He can't look out for himself."

"Don't worry, I'm sure we'll soon find him. Can you think of anyone he might go to see, or anywhere he likes to go?"

She rattled her head from side to side. "He doesn't have anyone," she muttered. Sam saw the concern, the compassion, in this woman's face. She cared. "I don't know where he'd go, but tonight is the Perseids."

"The what?"

"The Perseid meteor shower," she clarified. "Ambrose is obsessed with star gazing. He gets really excited whenever there's an eclipse, or a meteor shower. And he took his telescope, so…"

"OK," Sam made a note.

"So, we think we know what he's doing. It still doesn't help figure out where he'd go."

Mrs Quince shrugged apologetically.

"I guess he'll want somewhere away from the lights of the city. But where exactly, I have no idea."

"Can you describe what he was wearing?"

"Yes," she ticked off on her fingers.

"Jeans, a grey shirt, a yellow waistcoat, and a red cowboy hat."

Sam thought she'd misheard. "A cowboy hat?"

"Red," confirmed Mrs Quince. "Oh, and my suitcase is missing. But all of Ambrose's belongings are still in his room. Except for the telescope of course. He must be using the case for that."

"OK, can you describe the suitcase?"

~ * ~

Ambrose had made decent time. It must be years since he'd ventured into the heart of Birmingham. He'd worried he might lose his way. Ridgemont was in Edgbaston, nestled in quiet back streets just on the skirts of the city. Ambrose had played it safe, cutting through nearby residential areas until he came upon the Hagley Road, where soon enough he'd been able to hop a bus to the centre.

Disembarking in Broad Street he looked around, startled for a moment by the changes about him. Jostled by other passengers spilling out onto the pavement, Ambrose hurried to get out of the way, pulling a pink suitcase after him with a distinctive squeak. He scanned the horizon. He knew what he was looking for. Or at least, he was sure he'd know it when he saw it. But here. So many people! The bustle of the day didn't diminish with the onset of evening. Rather it grew, multiplying as the numerous bars and restaurants drew swarms of customers, eagerly buzzing around, ready to sample the nectar on offer. Ambrose found it fascinating. But also confusing. Lots of noise made his head hurt, and scrambled his concentration like runny eggs. He began to regret getting off the bus so soon, but had feared losing his bearings.

Best to keep moving, he decided.

With much weaving, dodging, and 'xcuse me's, he gradually escaped the crush of humanity heading for a night out. Finding some space he paused to get his breath, gawping open-mouthed at a strange swirly building; large cubes smothered in many circles. It turned out to be the library.

"Huh!" said Ambrose, and went on his way.

Trotting into the shadow of the museum, pink suitcase rattling along behind on wobbly wheels, he pulled his pocket watch from his waistcoat. It wasn't strictly speaking a real pocket watch, just an old digital Casio with a broken strap. But he'd secured it with a piece of blue string and thrilled in retrieving it with a flourish to check his progress. It had been a couple of hours since he'd left Ridgemont Care Home.

Victoria Square opened out at his feet. Here there were less people - which was good, but it was too open, too exposed. And whilst the pale stone and gracious columns of the museum and council house were at least familiar, they wouldn't serve his purpose tonight.

The day was nearly done, and Ambrose felt the burden of fatigue after his daring flight from Ridgemont. He decided to rest up until the final rays of the sun had slipped away.

Soon enough he found a quiet place. A narrow alley, encumbered with overflowing bins, scaffolding and stacks of wooden pallets. Here evening already settled into hidden pools. Ambrose ventured halfway down, found a place against the wall where he set his case and sat down gratefully, leaning against the pink plastic and rubbing tired knees. With a low grumble in his belly he fleetingly regretted missing dinner. Tonight was banana fritters for afters. But, this was more important.

With a weary sigh he examined his immediate surroundings.

71

Several feet away lay a misshapen bundle of clothing. He thought he detected movement and for a moment feared rats (or worse!).

The pile of clothes turned out to be named Brian.

Waiting for the last vestiges of the day to leach away, Ambrose and Brian shared a can of warm Sprite and their views on the city's best vantage points to view the Perseids.

"Why head into the city at all though?" asked Brian, - not for the first time. He blinked at the old man squatting next to him. "Isn't there too much light?"

Ambrose chuckled at Brian's stupidity. "The meteor shower is in the sky, my friend. The closer I get to the sky, the better I'll be able to see. Just need to find a high place."

Brian's brow contracted beneath his hoodie. "I think your logic might be flawed, old boy."

He got a finger waggled in his face. "My logic is quite sound."

Ambrose fumbled for the Casio on its string again. "Time's getting on."

Struggling to his feet he grasped Brian's hand, giving it a friendly squeeze. Then he was off, dragging the pink suitcase back along the alley and squeaking off into the night.

Brian watched him go, pulling his jacket a little tighter as the first evening chills crept into his bones.

~ * ~

The end of the working day. The usual press of humanity. Heads down, swift feet, a polite stampede to get out of the city. Trams and trains and buses stopped and started, the squash of commuters interchanging at each crowded stop.

Others flocked to the city's bars instead. Unravelling the day with wine and cocktails, deflating their tensions with alcohol, friends, flirting, before they too would steer homeward.

Olivia Dawson fell into neither category. She was one of the dedicated souls working late. Or so it appeared. The office rapidly emptied around her. One or two other intrepid colleagues lingered for a while, some working, and some just chatting. Eventually they too left, one by one. As nine o'clock approached Olivia stretched and looked around. She was alone in the office now; had been for some time. The motion activated, power-saving, lighting had blinked out in most areas, leaving her in a lone island of illumination, penned in by shadows. She closed her eyes, listened to the depth of silence. Other than the hum of air conditioning the office was quiet and still. Olivia was still too. She sat there for so long, immobile, a statue in a lemon blouse and navy skirt, that finally the last light in the office blinked off.

When she eventually opened her eyes she saw that beyond the darkness there were myriad lights outside the windows. The city winked at her a thousand times. It sparkled.

Out there was life. Happiness and adventure and love.

But Olivia could only observe from afar, locked inside her own misery. She'd taken such things for granted. Plodded oblivious through life, thinking she was just normal. The job, the home, the husband, the friends and family and all the frilly social clutter. Just normal, right? Now she knew she hadn't been normal. She'd been lucky.

As each segment had shrivelled away it left an ever widening void. Now Olivia was trapped in that void. Her cries were swallowed by its brutal hollowness, her tears turned to ice by the heartache. Olivia had tried to keep on being normal. She played the part, but now she was an actor trying to fool the world. Every day felt less real. The last thing she'd tried to hold onto was her dignity. But that was a brittle, foolish thing. She'd carried it around for some time, but now understood it was too weak to hold back the sucking vacuum.

Time to face the truth.

Darkness followed her. Taking the stairs she left behind the empty, shadowy office.

She left behind her laptop. She left behind her handbag. She left behind her keys, her purse. She left behind her wedding ring.

All she had with her was her mobile phone. She planned to send a text message.

Just one.

In the stairwell she peered down, looking over the sweep of railing. From here it was a plunging tunnel of blackness. She was a long way up. But not high enough. She felt the walls pressing in on her; the air was too thick and heavy in her lungs. Olivia swiped a tear angrily from her cheek and began her ascent. There were several more floors and a lot of steps before she made it to the top. She felt her thighs tighten with the effort but didn't slow her pace. The momentum felt important; the tap of her footsteps, the rhythm of her breathing, the pumping of her arms. She had purpose. She didn't want to lose this momentum, to lose this feeling.

Her feet didn't pause until she was right at the top. Olivia finally halted, gasping and shaking. Once the tremors subsided she reached for the door handle.

~ * ~

Brian had a knack for making himself comfortable, despite concrete beneath his backside, regardless of weather (except in the extremes), even tuning out the noise of traffic, shoppers, and drunks. Usually he was a contented little bug snuggled in his own cocoon.

But now he was uneasy.

He'd enjoyed chatting to the old fella. The guy was a bit of an odd ball, no question. But a gentle, charismatic, utterly generous and open-spirited oddball. He said his name was Ambrose – even his name was warm and charming.

Watching the sweet old guy wander off, humming quietly to himself, with a pink suitcase bumping along behind him and a loop of string dangling from his pocket, Brian couldn't avoid the prick of fear poking at his conscience.

Ambrose just looked so innocent, so clueless, and so utterly damned vulnerable.

The possibilities of what might happen were making Brian squirm, tilting his equilibrium, spoiling his comfort. He grumbled to himself, fretting in his dark corner, for several minutes. Finally, with a brief expletive but a good heart, Brian hoisted himself from his nest and set off.

The city was still in its transitional phase of the evening. Not many drunks yet. But a few. Always a few. A few shoppers too, flitting to and fro in the Bullring. But the streets weren't as crowded now. Brian preferred it when it was busy, chaotic even. He was invisible then. The very denseness of humanity shielded him. But the next few hours were uncertain, and he felt exposed, especially away from his usual spot.

Ambrose spoke of getting up high. Brian followed his nose, and the skyline, hoping to stumble across the dear old boy. After half an hour, during which he dodged a couple of sketchy characters, he began to feel like giving up. He could wander around all night and never find who he was looking for. Without a better idea of where Ambrose was going it was a fruitless search.

He felt bad for letting him go off alone, into the city, now bathed in streetlamps and artificial light. He glanced up at the sky. He could only see darkness above the illuminated streets of Birmingham. Maybe Ambrose would look at this same patch of sky. Come to the same realisation.

Brian was about to turn round and go back to his spot, when

he spotted a familiar hat. A red, slightly battered, cowboy hat.

~ * ~

"They're starting early tonight," grumbled Harry.

They'd just got a report of a disturbance on Colmore Row. Two guys had got into a fight. Sam was driving, pressed her foot a little harder. All they knew from the call was that it was two males.

"At least there'll be extra officers on duty this evening, what with the alert."

Harry tutted. "Another bloody alert. They're a waste of time."

Sam disagreed. "There have been incidents. The airlines are certainly taking them seriously, after all those navigational problems a couple of weeks ago."

"How can solar flares affect planes?" asked Harry, folding his beefy arms. "Especially at night. Bloody sun's gone down now!"

"Something to do with affecting the earth's magnetic field, I think," muttered Sam, her attention more on the road than Harry's scepticism.

"Just an excuse for overtime if you ask me."

Sam didn't respond this time. She'd been following the reports, the growing concern about outages, disruption, danger to the public. The solar flare activity was at an unprecedented high. Warnings were numerous, but, like Harry, most people had got used to the apparent scare mongering of the scientists. They weren't taking them seriously. Sam hoped tonight proved just as uneventful as the previous alerts.

Pulling up on Colmore Row, Sam got out the car, rested her knuckles on her hips, and took in the scene.

And it was a scene, rather than a fight. A homeless guy and a teenager were in a tug-of-war over a red, felt cowboy hat.

"Didn't Mrs Quince say our missing old guy wore a red hat?" asked Harry, appearing at her side.

She nodded, "But I don't see any sign of him. Come on."

They quickly broke the two of them apart. The kid was really drunk, talking gibberish and wafting the hat jubilantly. Having Harry loom over him sobered him slightly, enough for the constable to stop him jigging about and take the hat from him.

"Where did you get this, son?"

The lad's speech was so garbled Sam and Harry could only look at each other helplessly.

"It doesn't belong to him," piped up the homeless guy, who stood meekly next to Sam, but his voice had an angry edge. "That's Ambrose's hat." He pointed at the red hat now held in Harry's beefy paw.

"You know Ambrose Cotton?"

"Met him earlier. I was trying to find him. Worried about him out here alone. Especially with idiots like this about!"

Sam shared the guy's concern. "What's your name?"

"Brian."

"Hi, Brian. Did Ambrose say where he was heading?"

Brian shook his head sadly. "No, just that he was taking his telescope to watch some meteor shower."

"What makes you think he'd come into the city centre?" she asked, thinking about what Mrs Quince had said about getting away from the lights of the city. "This must be the worst place for star gazing."

He shrugged. "That's what I said. But he insisted he'd get the best view if he found a high place. Sweet fella, but a bit tapped I'd say." Brian drummed a finger against his temple to highlight his point.

Sam gazed up and down the street, looked around at the buildings, shops, offices, cranes. There were so many high places. Though most would be secured. She was already mentally trying to break down the possibilities, to eliminate those that would be locked or guarded.

Then they were plunged into darkness.

~ * ~

Olivia Dawson stepped out onto the roof of her office building. She let the door softly click closed behind her. Stood still, enjoying the gentle buffeting breeze. It teased her hair, prickled her skin, and dried the tear tracks across her cheeks.

For weeks her mind had been in turmoil, her emotions pulled so tight she felt in constant fear of snapping. For the first time in a long time she experienced a moment of delicious calm.

Then the lights went out.

What the hell?

Despite standing on a dark rooftop, the power cut in the city all around her made a profound difference. For a second it was utterly disorientating. She felt adrift, upended, and horribly lonely. Her breathing became laboured again, this time from some deep-rooted primal fear in her belly. Suddenly she craved light, just a little, a tiny anchor to stop her spinning into nothingness. She felt the smoothness of the phone still gripped in her hand.

Of course!

Olivia quickly accessed her phone and selected the torch function. The bright, hazy beam suddenly blanketing her came as a relief. She almost smiled; an expression her face was unaccustomed to of late. There were probably hundreds of people doing the same thing all over the city. For a second she imagined a multitude of tiny lights bobbing around down there, finding their way to safety. But, up here, it was like no one else existed. With the torch to guide her way Olivia took a quick look around, then headed for the edge.

~ * ~

Ambrose had known tonight would turn out just fine. OK, so he'd lost his hat. That was a minor blow. He'd bought it on his last holiday. When was that? Last year? Ten years ago? The story of his life sometimes shifted like sand in his mind, making it hard to pinpoint people, events, and times. Still, he didn't need a hat tonight. As long as he had his telescope and a clear sky he was good to go.

He'd taken a few twists and turns to get as far as possible from the drunken young man who'd taken his hat. Some might consider themselves a bit lost, but Ambrose was on a mission. He followed the heavens. He stopped to take stock, thinking about where to go next, thinking about his adventure so far. The hat theft had been stressful, but he'd enjoyed his visit with Brian. It was nice to make a new friend. Brian had been a good listener, and when he talked to Ambrose he didn't speak loudly or slowly, as if talking to someone hard of hearing. Or stupid. Yes, Brian was a good sort. He hoped to see him again some time.

Time to look for a way up.

But every door Ambrose tried was locked, or brought stiff-faced security personnel telling him to 'move along'. He didn't despair. Despair wasn't in Ambrose Cotton's nature. Perseverance was. So he kept going, humming tunelessly with the case squeaking and bobbing in his wake. It felt close amongst the city streets. Ambrose stopped to dab at his brow with a handkerchief.

The sudden blackout only mildly startled him.

"What the Dickens?"

Then he looked up, and grinned a toothy smile in the darkness. With the world devoid of light, the stars were no longer shy. They stole from the sky to glint proudly down on Ambrose.

Then, another light caught his attention. This one wasn't light years away. This one was just above him, on the roof of a nearby building. It moved slowly, disappeared a couple of times, and then danced back into view.

It was a sign, he was sure of it.

He hurried across the street to a side door of the building with the bobbing light. The door opened smoothly for him. He stepped inside. He couldn't see a thing, so felt around, shuffling cautiously. His hand found a railing. His toe detected a step. Stairs! Ambrose still held the handle of the suitcase in his other hand. He'd have to carry it. But, why carry the case and the telescope? No. Better to take the telescope out and leave the case down here.

Chuckling happily, Ambrose propped the now empty pink case against the open door frame and, hoisting his prized telescope onto his shoulder, he began to climb the stairs.

~ * ~

The drunken teen had turned a corner in his inebriation. His high had reached its lofty peak and was now on a downward turn.

"I'd better stay with him, make sure he's alright," said Harry, watching the young man with undisguised disgust. "Maybe you should have a look around for the old guy."

Sam agreed. "Poor soul must be terrified, out there in the pitch black, all alone." She looked about, shining her police-issue torch up and down. "He can't have gone far," she said, more to herself than anyone. "We know he was right here not too long ago." Her observations were optimistic more than realistic, but she'd like to find him. Preferably before all the looters and opportunists came crawling from their holes.

"I'll help," offered Brian.

~ * ~

Olivia sat on the ledge. She switched off the torch. Then she began composing a text message. It was short. She'd already planned what to write. A balloon of sadness inflated in her chest as she typed the words. She re-read her message. She didn't want there to be any bitterness. Just love. A little regret perhaps, but no anger. Satisfied, she pressed 'send'. Placing the phone on the ledge next to her she took a long breath. The blackout had been a surprise. Not part of the plan. Now though, it felt like a blessing. She was all encased in the night. She couldn't see any distance in front, behind, or below. It would make it easier.

Olivia got to her feet.

Now or never.

~ * ~

The climb had been hard on Ambrose. The last few levels were a blur of pain for the old man. The weight of the telescope had become agony, pressing down on his weary bones, bruising the fragile skin around his shoulder blade.

Pure will carried him on. Though his limbs shook so badly he almost fell more than once, he couldn't stop. If he paused for a moment he may not be able to get going again. He just had to get to the top. This must be the right place. Why else would there have been a beacon to guide him? Ambrose had long since stopped trying to steer the course of his fate. He'd kept getting lost that way; kept drifting into miserable cul-de-sacs. He chose instead to ride the waves of chance. He always looked for signs. A bright light high up in a dark city was as clear a sign as there could be. So his trembling legs would just have to get him to that roof.

When he finally burst through the door at the top he was gasping and wheezing violently. He dropped to his knees, groaning as they struck the ground. Ambrose carefully laid down the telescope, gentler with that than with his own meagre frame.

He needed a moment to recover. He'd made it to the top. Better to let the shaking subside before attempting to set up his equipment. To break his precious reflector now would be tragic.

Ambrose blinked. The darkness here was softer than the black hole of the stair well. Cool air revived him a little, enough to look around, trying to make sense of shadows hidden within shadows.

Soon he believed he could make out the edge of the roof. At first he thought his blurry eyes were playing tricks on him. But then he frowned. Was something moving over there?

~ * ~

Despite Sam's diligence and the powerful torch she carried, it was Brian who spotted the suitcase, propped just inside an open door. Sam shone a light inside.

"Stairs," declared Brian. "He must be up there."

"Hold on." She focussed on the pink case first, checking inside.

"Empty, of course," Brian said excitedly, eager to get going.

Sam shone her torch up into the stairwell. "AMBROSE," she called out. Her own voice echoed eerily back down to her. She listened for a moment, hoping for a reply, not really expecting one.

"OK, I guess we're going up."

She'd just reached the third floor when her radio crackled. It was Harry.

"Say again," Sam spoke urgently into the handset. "Are you sure, about the location? I'm in that building now."

With sinking heart she listened to his confirmation. A concerned citizen had received a disturbing text from his ex-wife. This news added to Sam's burden. There was more than one vulnerable person to worry about tonight.

She glanced up. Brian lumbered several steps ahead of her, persevering in his eagerness, even though she carried their only light. He wanted to find Ambrose. So did she. But what awaited them on that rooftop?

Dashing off fears and doubt, Sam got moving. She forced a quicker pace than before, despite her tired legs and searing lungs. In moments she'd overtaken Brian.

"Where's the fire?" he called to her rapidly retreating back, but she didn't answer. She needed each and every ounce of breath.

~ * ~

Ambrose blinked rapidly but couldn't penetrate the utter darkness. Still, he felt a presence.

"Hello?"

A voice warbled, emotion-fuelled. Fearful? The voice was female.

"Don't mind me," Ambrose assured the woman on the roof. "Just here for the Perseids." Testing his legs, he managed to stand. Still a little wobbly but feeling better, he propped his hands on his hips and looked around. It was still too dark to see much of anything. He cast his gaze skyward instead; smiled at the friendly stars. Stepping away from the doorway he found some space, explored gingerly, arms feeling for

83

obstacles, feet tentative. He felt the ledge running around the edge of the roof. It was deep, a few feet wide. That would be perfect. Excitement energised him, and he hurried to fetch the telescope.

He set the tripod on the corner ledge, then, picking up the telescope, he climbed up next to the tripod, and began attaching it to the base.

Light steps approached. "What are you doing?" Same voice as before, still fearful, but the tone of the fear was different somehow.

"Hello, my dear," he greeted, still focussed on assembling his pride and joy. "Apologies, tricky work in the dark. But then, the dark is the point, isn't it?"

"I have a light, if it helps?"

Ambrose considered. If he didn't set up the scope right it might detach; could fall and break. "Um, yes. I think that would be a good idea. Thank you."

When the small torch blinked on the brightness was like a blast of light after so long in the dark. Ambrose blinked, stumbled, his hand instinctively moving to shield his eyes. Ambrose's balance abandoned him, his tired legs fumbled for control. He caught a glimpse of the edge, over the edge. He sensed the drop, the deep space falling away beneath him. Ambrose cried out as he felt himself lurching towards the abyss.

Then, arms were around his waist. He was pulled to safety, lifted off the ledge and back onto the rooftop.

The light had fallen to the ground. It lit them up from its place by their feet. Ambrose looked into the eyes of his saviour. Large, dark and sad. He saw mascara streaks. She'd been crying.

"All's well now," he assured, patting her shoulder. "Well, must get back up there. The Perseids wait for no man."

"Let's put the telescope on the roof instead," she suggested. "You'll be able to see just as well. The ledge isn't safe."

Ambrose cocked his head and considered her logic. "Perhaps you're right."

Together they lifted down the scope, setting the tripod safely on the roof.

"It must have been your light I saw from the street," Ambrose said, checking all was secure. "You guided me here. You're my guardian angel, my dear." Ambrose gave her his toothiest grin. Olivia looked into the old man's face, lit up with more than torchlight. It shone with uncomplicated joy. Despite herself she smiled back at him, the weight in her heart eased, just a little.

"Actually," she said. "I think you're mine."

~*~

When Sam and Brian burst breathless through the door, Ambrose and Olivia were huddled around the telescope. Ambrose straightened.

"Put out that blasted light!" he yelled at Sam, then. "Oh, Brian! Hello, my friend."

Sam, exhausted, slid to the floor, reached for her radio. Her voice tremulous but relieved, "Found them," she said. "They're fine. They're both fine."

The City Pubs at Night

Alistair Matthews

Monday 5th February **Lost and Found**

If you are looking for a night out drinking in Birmingham, then you cannot find a grander pub than the Lost and Found. On entering you find yourself swallowed up in a huge hall with a mixture of modern and Victoriana artwork adorning the walls. The ceiling is somewhere up in the heavens where chandeliers hang suspended. For sheer size there is no larger conventional drinking premises in the city.

It is not quite a conventional pub in its layout, as a restaurant section is on a raised level. This is accessed by a few steps, to the right of the bar area as you step through the revolving glass door frontage. The bar itself sells a range of excellent ales and ciders; all from English breweries I'm glad to say. Reasonably priced as well, considering this pub lies on Bennetts Hill, coming off New Street, which is the main street in the centre of Birmingham.

The building itself has a history of transformation. When I first visited ten years ago the same venue was called "Bennetts". My mother told me that before it was ever a pub it was a bank, the National Westminster. It had provided her with her first job as a clerk when leaving school. To the left of the bar area there is a door that opens on to a meeting room with a large square table and chairs that no doubt catered for the bank's board of directors back in the day. Nowadays this room can be booked for an hourly fee and is popular with various clubs, societies and businesses. Indeed, the clientele of the pub this evening seems to have a large business person contingent.

It is an appropriate venue for my companion of the evening. Karen works for HSBC like me, although on a lower managerial scale to myself. At 26, she has aspirations to progress further, taking an MBA course at the weekends. We sit at a table for two in the corner and converse. I talk about the pub and its décor and history but she is more into talking about work and the establishment where we have our travail.

She strikes me as being well held in emotionally. Gives little away about her likes and dislikes. She came to meet me in the pub straight from work, dressed in a trouser suit, with a red coat she has draped on the chair and a scarf to keep the cold out. She keeps her scarf on.

After half hour she says, "Excuse me, I have to contact someone," and pulls out her mobile.

Wednesday 7th February **Wellington**

If you continue up Bennetts Hill from the Lost and Found you come to another pleasant pub on the right, the Wellington. This has a plain décor, with nothing fancy or memorable on the walls. What is memorable is the friendly atmosphere. It has obvious regular customers who know each other and chat cheerfully to the bar staff and each other. It has some irregular customers as well. On previous occasions when I've dropped in I've spotted previous Lord Mayors of Birmingham. When the Lib-Dems held a conference in Birmingham a few years ago I saw the MP and well-known TV personality Lembit Opik having a drink with some companions.

The Wellington specialises in real ales, of which it has 17 different brews. These are displayed on a board and listed, so you can order at the bar by quoting a number. There are five traditional ciders and apparently over 150 whiskies. I once overheard a visitor from the Capital exclaim exuberantly, "They've got nothing like this in London!"

Perhaps it has always been a friendly pub. My mother told me she met my father for the first time in here, long before it became the specialist ale establishment it is now.

Back in 2014 the Wellington publican acquired rights to the vacant office spaces above it and set about a building conversion. There is now an outside terrace drinking space on the first floor, which is naturally not used much at this time of year. It is unique, I believe, in being the only pub in the centre of Birmingham that has a separate upstairs bar.

A fact I intimated to my companion of the evening. "I hope you don't mind heights," I quipped. We were in the lounge to the right of the bar that you reach once you have climbed the stairs. During the day, if you sit by the window you have an unusual and intimate view of the goings to and fro on Bennetts Hill. On this cold February night the view is somewhat dark.

Shirley smiled at my quip. She is an estate agent, and a successful one judging by her stylish bright yellow jacket. A good-looking dark haired woman about thirty. As to be expected, for the job she does, she talks glibly and incessantly. In fact she seems to me to be speaking a lot without really saying anything. It is unfortunate that early on after our meeting she mentions that she is married and has a child at home. I can't help thinking about the outcome of my mother meeting my father in this very place. It haunts the rest of the evening I spend with her.

Friday 9th February **The Square Peg**

This pub lies on Corporation Street, the second main thoroughfare of the city coming eastwards off New Street. It is a part of the Wetherspoons chain of brewery, so one can expect reasonably priced beer. Also, no ghastly music blaring out, which always spoils pubs for me. With its location it is always busy at any time of day. The clientele are homogenous: business people, shoppers, and visitors to Birmingham centre and what have you.

It occupies the first floor of an extremely tall building which used to be a department store called Lewis's, but that was before my time.

When the pub opened in the 1990's my mother worked as a barmaid there for a short time. She had lost her managerial job at Nat West, due to the breakdown in her marriage and her mental health.

Somebody once told me the Square Peg has the longest bar of any pub in Europe.

I do not know if that is true but it does stretch a bit and I quipped to my date for the night, "Thought I'd never find you."

She smiled.

Margaret is a plump blonde who works somewhere in the admin department of Birmingham Council. Her conversation jumps from subject to subject. She starts off telling me how boring her job is. We get on to The Great British Bake Off on TV, and somehow I end up learning what her favourite colour is. She commences on a long story about her boss who fancies her. He travels from Barnt Green to Birmingham city centre every day. His name is Raymond, or possibly Richard; I have stopped listening by then.

Perhaps it is partly due to the booze I have been imbibing this week but I feel fatigued and it is difficult to concentrate on what Margaret is saying. There is also a distraction with the low-cut black dress she is wearing. She has an ample bosom. I know I am losing my manners but I can't help but stare. I think she notices and smiles.

I snap out of it and turn my head. Glancing at the bar I see three of the staff leaning towards each other. They are talking and looking at me. A chill goes through me.

Saturday 10th February **Prince of Wales**

This pub is on Cambridge Street, which is not far from the nightlife sights of Birmingham. Symphony Hall, considered by some to have the best acoustics in the country, is a few hundred metres away. The canals of Birmingham are a similar distance in another direction. Cambridge Street lies parallel with Broad Street, which, with its pubs, clubs and casinos is the hub of Birmingham nightlife. However, Cambridge Street is a quiet street and this pub is like an oasis of peace in the hustle and bustle.

It is a small pub with just one bar. On a Saturday night it can be standing-room-only sometimes as a crowd of theatre goers invade. When the show is about to commence they move on and the pub becomes contrastingly empty.

This evening we have caught an empty period and are sat at a table in the corner. I explain to my companion in jocular fashion why I have preferred to meet up in this place,

"…. Centre of town getting too hot for me, so I decided to go away. 'Go West young man', as Horace Greeley once said. Ha! Whoever Horace Greeley was. Of course this pub isn't too far west from the centre of town. Ha,ha!"

"What the fuck are you talking about?" She says.

Kaye is a well-shaped girl in her 20's with dyed red hair. She wears a tight miniskirt despite the cold outside. She works for Network Rail in some capacity. I'm not sure what capacity; I am now finding it difficult to follow her conversation. The boozing I have been doing recently is now really starting to catch up with me. What is clear to me is that

Kaye has had a few drinks before we even met up. Our initial conversation I took to be just silly chatter coming from her but now a new, more vulgar Kaye has emerged.

I apologise, "I dunno," and shrug my shoulders. She continues chattering and I slump back in my chair, a complete blank.

I am startled out of my semi stupor when she says; "I haven't had a shag for two years."

I stare at her. I do not know what my face looks like. She then giggles, turns her head and repeats loudly to the room, "I haven't had a shag for two years!"

People in the small pub turn and look. People on the stools by the bar. On the tables, they all turn and look. I had thought of coming here to avoid attention. So much for that.

I think of a quip, "You say you work for Network Rail. Strikes me you've gone off the rails."

She stares at me with drunken eyes. The stare turns into a glare as it dawns on her that I am deprecating her.

Sunday morning 11th February

I have just got out of bed. Head aching. Still in my pyjamas I have made my way to the kitchen and brewed a cup of tea. I sit and look out the window at the light dawning over Birmingham. This house where I have lived all my life stands on a hill with a view of the city centre high building outline six miles away. The silence is disturbed by the sound of cars drawing up outside. There is another brief silence, then a loud knocking at the door. I remain seated but the shock of the noise jolts my aching head to thought. The thought is, women, women, if not for -

"Police, open up!"

(Extract from Birmingham mail 12ᵗʰ February)

House of Horror

The bodies of four women have been found in a house at West Heath

Police arrest a man

…. John Curbishley, who lives in a neighbouring house, said, "This has always been a quiet area. You never think anything like this is going to happen round here….

(Extract from Birmingham prison psychiatrist report. 27ᵗʰ June)

…. The facts of this case can be briefly summed up. Lampard arranged dates with women through a matchmaking app.. After meeting them in public houses in the centre of Birmingham he offered them lifts home and whilst in the car he bludgeoned them to death. This case at first sight bears a resemblance to that of Philip Smith, a 35-year-old taxi driver, who murdered three women in Birmingham over a four-day period in November 2000. However, unlike Smith, whose motives for the murders are unclear, it can be strongly speculated that the origins of Lampard's actions arose from the death of his mother four months previously. The inmate is a single man who, at 28, had lived alone with his mother all his adult life. Although I have found it difficult to illicit lengthy responses of any depth on the character of his mother I can gather clues as to how the bereavement derailed his life psychologically.

Lampard has no previous criminal record. He lived what appears to have been a respectable life, with a managerial job in Admin at the HSBC bank.

My impression of Lampard is coming across as amiable and jovial at times. Whilst obviously a danger to women, non violent as far as this institution is concerned.

When asked about how he felt being in prison he said he was amenable, but he would miss the pubs of Birmingham....

The Mummers' Boy

Mat Joiner

1.

There he lies – Stonegalleon, my shattered son – in a ditch by the train track, the pretty angles of his face all askew. Blood rills through his hair, masks the eyes he liked to paint with rust or oil, that flashed any colour they could steal.

I could make every mouth at my disposal mourn him; but I won't share this grief. Imagine, my citizens, that the ground squirming underfoot is a mere quake – you will never know the *why* of it. I could rend myself apart, brick to dust, for this. I will not.

I gather my Mummers, the ghosts that delighted the boy not so long ago. Wreathe him in goldenrod, willowherb, and buddleia. A star torn from beer cans on his forehead, a shroud of maps to keep him warm. Through the one Stonegalleon called the Banshee, I howl my loss.

A train rackets past (how he loved to race these machines; never again). Maybe its passengers take my song for gulls and sirens, see the mourners as rags sucked up in the train's wake.

They scud onto some place not me, unknowing.

The Mummers dance a tattered ballet, in arcs of grief; and then I disperse them forever.

Later, vagrants will steal into the ditch, gaze in wonder on his wrecked beauty. Then they will burn him. I would not have him as carrion. They will daub his ashes on their tongues, and in nights to come, there will be stories of him, of a city and its boy.

I didn't see his birth, or his mother laying him on a gashed and filthy mattress. I heard him squalling: my streets there on the eastern edge were thin and tenantless. I noticed how rats and foxes had gathered by a long-shuttered, crack-windowed factory. The beasts drew closer. It would be a swifter end than exposure, if little meat for any of them; but it was curious, seeing them gathered like that. I watched with blear-glass eyes.

He stopped crying. His eyes caught what light there was. A chubby fist waved, then opened. He was *beckoning* them, it seemed. They padded around him in circles, puzzled and enthralled, making no move to attack. What was this thing up to?

I bade a fox pick him up by the scruff of his neck. He dangled, as goblin-like as any other baby, except for his eyes: they were focussed, trapping what light there was, and they saw *me*. Not my hide of tumbledown warehouses and swollen churches: me.

I pondered. Should I let the animals have their feast? What was this foundling to me? Yet he'd been laid on my doorstep, and he was not quite *empty*. Whatever was there – not yet person or power – could be shaped. *I could build him.* I'd seen thousands of humans raise their young; how difficult could it be for me?

So I made my decision.

2.

I named him Stonegalleon, from the chipped factory sign above his birth-bed; later, he called himself *Galley*. Vixens suckled him. Rats and pigeons brought him the richest scraps until he was old enough to forage for himself. On winter nights, cats were his blankets. He began to merge with his foster-family: squabbling with the other cubs, his hair grew russet; the bones of his face yearned for a muzzle. Among the rodents, his eyes were beady-black, and he held his food in little paws. I wouldn't let him slip into beasthood. He needed tutelage. So I wove the Mummers for him, out of rags and memories, robed them in dustbin bags and cast-off shadows. I made him three:

The Cartographer, with its mask of A to Zs and newsprint and its street-lit eyes. The edgelands haunter, guide to streets demolished, half remembered. I led Nettler through the tweenstreets, the hollow ways, taught him to open doors to uncommon land, bunkers, ghost parks, streets I'd folded away from everyday sight. *I am not frozen music,* I told him; *I am thawed.*

The Dredger, the angel of canals, lost rivers, standing waters. A gorgon's head of moss and streaming weed. Dank and lapping kisses I gave him brought him jewels from sewers and unlikely things thought drowned forever. I let him scry silted and peacock-slicked mirrors. Futures torqued, sideshow cities.

The Banshee, my spokesthing – an eyeless being, face a white trumpet like a great bindweed flower. I had a plethora of voices, scrounged, found (there are fossil sounds everywhere). I sang the infant Galley lullabies, the soft rumble of distant traffic; scolded him with words of shattered glass. I lectured him while he caught and ate woodlice. His first words were written in beetles' blood. There are runes, neon spoor, all over my walls if you choose to see – his testament.

He had favourite places. The canal junction he called "the Bridge of Eyes" for its curious graffiti. He cut roads into the dark ziggurat of the library, stalking its shelves deep into the night. A cinema fronted by dummies (harlequins, ringmasters, unlikely lovers) in alcoves; he stole one of the mannequins, shunting it from place to place until I made him replace it. And the overgrown spot on the bank of one of my waterways he found when he was thirteen – hardly more than a trickle in a brick trench – a place where escaped garden flowers grew. Among the lupins and balsam, men came to fuck at dusk. Stonegalleon watched them, his pupils huge, hand working between his legs.

He filched elements from all these places to make a den – a variegated ugliness, part hunched bridge, part warped tree, carapaced with car-shells. I didn't come there, often. I imagine him playing with the fancy pigeons and oxidised keys he loved then, library books turning to mulch under his bare feet. In his teens, he became ambitious. Blind spots appeared all over me, from which he wouldn't emerge for days, weeks.

This upset me. I was family. There was nothing we hadn't shared. I had put him to sleep, then taken him *inside* me, dissolved him into the streetplan, the waterways. He knew what it was to have a gabled skull and solid foundations, each car on his roads like a fleeting thought, to have a skin of sandstone and asphalt. In turn, I wore his flesh. Such a fragile thing. (Citizens, you helped make me, but I find it hard to credit.) I was crammed into this meat-being, surely it would burst. I took one step after another, attempted speech like a drunkard. Heady, this, but I could not be so small now. We met on the way back to our rightful bodies: a brief sweet fusion. You could not tell who was the brick, who the mortar.

3.

I have so many questions now.

Tell me: did you see my Galley as he went about his travels?

97

From the edge of your eye? Some twist of static on the security monitor, as he slid and out of the High Street bazaars? (A greatcoat to wear, then candies and tinselled lipstick to fill its pockets. He wears it still, on his pyre.)

Perhaps you heard him in the small hours, running with his fox-cousins for old times' sake. Or you heard of a red-headed child squatting in front of a condemned high-rise, scowling and biting his lip as he willed the building to twist out of all recognition. Then he would wait for me to make the next move. This was the Tower Game. I'd subtract a floor. He'd overplay, make the tower wear its own staircase like a feather boa. The loser, of course, was the one to bring it down in dust; it was almost always him. Oh, he was strong, but I was old and cunning.

Maybe you were in the club on the waterside, the old factory, where the bass loosened bone from skin. Stonegalleon was there too. Did you flinch as he danced through you; take the flail of him for shadows and strobes? His beats weren't yours: he danced to a rough music, the clank and judder of machines long gone.

The homeless knew him, a little. Drawn by the wasteland fires, bodies in sleeping bags (he thought they were pupating) he came to talk. He gave them a poetry they didn't understand, Tarot readings from shards of stained glass, a gargoyle he'd improvised from a gull turned inside-out (still alive – just, and keening), studded with clinker. Nothing they wanted. Some worshipped Galley, which puzzled and frightened him; others drove him out with fists and curses.

Tell me, though I'm only your city and you cannot hear: would it have gone differently if I'd not hoarded him, and he'd had some measure of quotidian things? Did he hanker for friends, lovers, and a roof over his head that was only a roof? After all the wonders I showed him.

There are others cities than you. He said that to me, and at first it was not a challenge.

I never denied it. Cities wiser, older, and prettier than me, some who *care* for their people! It didn't bother me. We are by nature solitary beings. I never thought Galley might want to *see* them.

I had dismantled his blind spots one by one. I didn't find him in any of them; he was instead zigzagging around my very borders, looking for weak spots. At last I came upon him trudging the motorway verges. I gave him nausea at the thought of leaving me, made him retch, and implanted the idea that he'd die beyond my limits. *These "other cities" won't want you. They'll chew you up and spit out the pips. You'll be nothing to them. Stay where you're wanted.* But he carried on, puking until he was hollow. He even stuck out his thumb, as if any sane driver would be able to see him, let alone willingly give him a ride. I made the traffic seem like a metal tide, ready to crush him, and still he walked. Only when I had tied the roads in a knot, bending all ways home, did he give in.

I let him shudder and sob in one of the old bunkers. I sent the Banshee to coo over him. I stroked his brow with underground draughts. He will be well soon, I thought, and there'll be no more of this.

Galley's next attempt was mundane and audacious. He simply tried to board a train. I didn't recognise him at first; he had done a good job of disguising himself − stealing the scent off one man, the bone structure from another, and so on. I only knew him because the end result felt to me like a jigsaw rather than a real human. Under my influence, the station crowd squeezed him, driving him towards the exit. He resisted for a few moments, trying to summon the gravity and weight of the building itself to push him onto the platform. In the end, I had to invert the station and throw him out bodily.

After that, I seeded all my stations with auras of unwelcome. I even hexed the bus stops. I should have gone further, reached inside Galley's head and ripped out the idea of elsewhere. I should never have told him I was a mere city, but the very universe.

I should have let him go.

But I did, in my way.

My police: did the graffiti this summer puzzle you? Who would take time to *burn* slogans into walls? Surely such a painstaking vandal could be caught. And what did these phrases mean - YOU LIVE IN A JEALOUS CITY, AGAINST INVISIBLE LIMITS, and the like. Some obscure protest. Two of us knew what it meant.

He mocked me with his train-racing, making the tweenstreets follow the track, emerging to scorch his name on a carriage, or frighten the passengers by leaving an indent of his face in window glass. How you flew, Galley, never quite trying to get on board, always doubling back before the train left town. He'd perch on a particular footbridge – the place where I found him tonight – and watch it go.

There was one coming now, out of the sunset. He was very still, hunched over. I had never seen that expression on his face before: longing and despair. It changed when he knew I was there – I had come as the Banshee, though I was silent – his face curdled. He looked at me as you would at a toy you'd outgrown. Tired and disgusted. CHEAP GHOST, he wrote into the bridge. Then he turned his back on me. I was silent when I embraced him. He stiffened with shock, then I said into his ear, "Travel then," (I do not know what voice I used: perhaps them all) and I threw him from the bridge.

He hit the carriage roof – I heard his bones snap, even over the wheels, and half his face was torn away – rolled and bounced into the ditch. Now, I thought, you'll learn. He was bent in all the wrong places, a shape from which no human, even my son, could return. It was only then I realised all I had done.

I have sent him into the greatest city of them all.

100

The Only Living Boy

from Tile Cross

David Croser

If the eye is supposed to catch the final image of a dying person - what about a *window*?

There were certainly a lot of them round Brindley Place, all seeming to stare back at him, reflecting him back again and again and again. Too many for a boy from Tile Cross having had one too many. And the rest. The dealer he'd got the pills from wasn't too specific about what they were called but had gone to great lengths to describe their effect. Again and again the windows reflected and repeated his image, caught in shades of neon and grey and amber, shadows deep and sharp on raw Birmingham November night. A thousand Kyes reflected back at him and every one of them laughing at him, mocking him, jeering at them for the fool he was. Not just a fool. Filthy. Sick. Diseased.

Kye stumbled away from them, up towards the fountain, a series of stepped pools with a flight of steps between them. He tried not to look down either side at the water lest reflections swim up from the depths to mock him, calling him all the names booming round his head.

Even the wind, the raw impersonal wonderfully indifferent wind, wasn't loud nor cold enough to drown them.

At the top of the steps Kye stopped, swaying, clutching his knees.

He was shaking and the twisting in his stomach made him so want to throw up. If only such a simple mechanical action could rid him of what he felt, what he was now. He heaved, once twice, coughing, retching, but nothing came but a string of snot and saliva and the bitter taste of reflux and the pavement bucked and swayed beneath his feet. He stayed that was till the feeling passed and revelers pushed past him heedless.

He was facing the canal. It was nearly midnight and an hour before he had been sitting in a bar on Broad Street, been there since six o'clock in the evening. In spite of the noise and the bustle he'd taken the last of the pills and somehow fallen asleep in a booth, a three quarter drunk lager as flat and lifeless as he felt on the table in front of him. Twice he'd been awoken by sudden cry or shout of another customer, once one of the bar staff to see if he wanted another, and once by a woman dressed as Wonder Woman and a big L plate round her neck who fell into his booth, her drink splattering the seat beside him. Her heavy breasts swung across his face as she fumbled to get up and join the rest of the hen night. He was so tired; he had felt so low that he scarcely had the energy to be angry. He gritted his teeth and pushed her upright. She wandered off. Getting up himself he'd stumbled out of the bar and into the street. He'd realised too late, as he passed the bouncers that he wanted to pee. And he was skint. And he had nowhere to go.

Standing by the Brindley Place fountain a couple passed him by, giving him a look. Kye turned, pulling up his coat collar while the wind nibbled delightedly at him through his light summer jeans, and started down past Café Rouge

103

towards the canalside. He had contemplated keeping on going and let the canal take him, but he had enough common sense left to realise it would be too busy. Too likely some idiot would grab him and pull him out. He decided instead to walk up as far as a certain bar he knew and look in. Maybe someone would see him and recognise him, maybe someone would give him as tenner, enough for a burger or maybe the price of an taxi back to Tile Cross, for services rendered. At the same time he hoped he wouldn't be recognised. Never again.

The canalside was quiet, as he descended, turning down towards Gas Street basin. Here and there someone passed him by, a lot of them couples. Those he tried hardest to ignore. As he came out under the canal bridge there was a knot of bright, white, chattering customers spilling out of the canal side pub.

The pubs neon name challenged the starless sky. The canal boats clustered across the dull water in the canal basin, unlit, blunt like so many dead things, belly up. He stared at them. Without meaning to, he caught his own expression reflected in the water, and saw someone reflected behind him. Kye turned and saw who it was.

Of course.

"A good try," said Jake.

"You still feeling sorry for yourself?" he said.

Kye shrugged, and turned away from the canal back.

"I only went to the bog."

Kye walked off along the towpath in the direction of the Mailbox.

"You can't keep avoiding me," said Jake, catching up and falling into step with him. In the darkness it was hard to see the expression on Kye's face nor his features. The stretch of towpath from the Broad Street to the Mailbox, though busy, even towards midnight, was sparsely lit. As much as the center of Birmingham could ever be in darkness, the occasional lights accentuated the flinty November night. A sharp wind made the filthy flat surface of the canal shudder, faint dull colours splintering and coalescing. At one point they were both in relative darkness and alone on the towpath. Jake grabbed Kye's arm.

"We've got to talk things through."

Kye pulled his arm back.

"What's there to talk about?"

He stared at the path, slick and iridescent with rain. He pushed Jake back against the wall. For a moment they were up close, close enough to feel their breath on each other's cheeks. For a moment Kye saw himself reflected in the other man's eyes. He recoiled, staggering back towards the canal's edge.

It was Jake's turn to grab him, and to pull instead of push, and drag him over to a bench against the wall. There was a lamppost next to the bench and just a little further back an archway lead back up onto Gas Street. The lamppost was one of the old fashioned sort, meant to look like a gas lamp. Its pale sickly pool of light was giving a fair imitation, and flickered as the wind caught the lamppost, making it shiver. The two men sat there, gasping for breath.

Jake still held onto Kye's arm but it felt limp. For the moment the fight had gone from him.

"Leonie's worried abut you. She's nearly called the cops twice already."

"Waste of her time."

"She's wanted to report you missing. Not – not anything else," said Jake

"She's your sister."

"And you're both in this together, mate."

Kye went to get up, stumbled, fell back on the hard, cold bench. He swore.

"What's wrong?"

"Sat on me bollocks."

Jake laughed. "Clumsy sod. How much you had?"

Kye clutched his head in his hands.

"Not enough. Never gonna be enough."

Jake sighed, putting an arm around the other man's shoulder.

"A mess, yeah. But not worth getting yourself like this, man."

"I've got Aids and we did it without protection. How the fuck is that not a mess?"

Jake took out a pack of cigarettes and offered it to his friend.

"You're HIV poz. You're on meds. She's always known that. Hasn't stopped you making a go of things. That night - you were both wasted. You fucked up. *Both* of you, man."

Kye crushed the cigarette packet in his hand.

"Not her. Me."

Jake prised the crumpled packet from his hand.

"Both of you. I don't know what's worse: listening to you trying to be the big macho man taking the blame - or your self pity."

"I'm not – "

"Don't try kidding me, Kye. Me of all people."

Jake reached out and took the other man's hand in his.

"Least when you were shagging me you weren't acting the big kid."

Kye turned away, his voice catching.

"I'm in such a mess, Jake."

Jake sighed. "Yes. But you can't sort it out by getting wasted and chucking yourself in the canal."

"You did," said Kye.

Jake shrugged.

"Look where it got me. I'm dead. I'm only here now 'cause you're off your head on pills."

Jake nodded towards a couple passing by on the way down to the lights and the sounds of the Mailbox.

"All they can see is you taking to yourself. Think they care? Another pissed up crackhead. The world's like that. It only cares if you make it care. You've got to make some light in the darkness, otherwise that's all there is. You come from nothing and you go back to nothing unless you make some light in the dark."

Jake looked up into the night sky. Somewhere, above the city, past the streetlights, above the mosaic of windows and cars and bars and phones, reflected back from cloud and a haze of mist and smoke, the silent stars went by.

"Leonie's pregnant. She doesn't know it yet but she will soon."

Kye stared at him.

"Never mind that you're poz. You're undetectable. You've both of you screwed up, but shit happens. She's gonna need you. The kid's going to need you: it's dad," said Jake.

Jake reached across, a hand brushing Kye's cheek. His lips brushed Kye's hand.

"Don't run away. Be the only living boy in Tile Cross, the one who says yes to life, however shitty it gets. It's easy to blame yourself or your status or other people. Take responsibility. Go back. Give them both a kiss for me."

Kye sat for a long time alone on the bench.

After a while the stars were hidden and the sky above clotted and it began to rain. The crowds towards Brindley Place and the Mailbox thinned and between them in the cold and the wet Kye sat staring at the canal, his hands working over the crushed packet of cigarettes. Idly he opened it.

Empty. Except – *A tenner?*

He frowned, pocketing the cash, and sighed. He walked over to the canal's edge. He stood there, looking down at the water, as still now as a mirror, reflecting his face back at him, without distortion or disturbance from wind or rain

Eventually he went through the passage onto Gas Street and out on to Broad Street to find a taxi: towards the light.Insert chapter nine text here.

The Wards of New Venice

Nicholas Doran

A report by Captain R.H. Vanderman of the Light Brigade Company. Commissioned by the Company's Centre Guildhall for the instruction of future recruits.

The isles of Birmingham are not for the unbloodied. I don't care if you've roughed it in the Londinium slums of Brentwood or the Rookeries of St. Albans; take a trip down Birmingham's canals after dark not mastered in the ways of a rifle alongside a company of five good men of likewise skill, and you'll soon be tasting it's soot and shit streaked waters before the night is done, *if you're lucky*. Still, most of you will likely be commissioned on guarding cargo through the wards before you even know the right way to *hold* a rifle so take this recount of mine as serious preparation if you want to stand even a farthing's chance of survival.

Got your attention? You'll likely die either way so I can only pray that these preambles warrant some dedication to memory the happenings I now put to paper.

Let us begin.

Despite the explosion of transit rails across our proud nation, the convention of canals has yet to abandon the commercialists' consciousness, with the blighted things slicing through our British Isles like some ungodly circulatory system. Of course with road journeying becoming so dangerous in recent decades across wasteland Britain, the byways prove to be a most convenient means of transportation for the poorer classes and for the less affluent commercial enterprises. This last one, alas, is where our services most often take us to the canals. For the cargo such companies transport proves to be a monopoly itself for the criminal underworld with the black wards of Birmingham at its dark heart.

You've doubtless heard the sayings *All roads lead to Jerusalem* and *All transit lines lead to Londinium.* Well, here's a third one for the ages, *All canals lead to Birmingham* and it's a phrase that marks the worst days of my career with Company quite neatly. Though I've always strived to make my way through Brum's byways during the pea-souped light of day, avoiding the worst of the city's homicidal menagerie, my latest contract necessitated travel under cover of night.

My squad consisted of two company members who I consider in the highest regard: Algernon A. Fadlan, a former TITAN militia veteran of the 12th West-Indian regiment; one of the sharpest eyed sentries and marksman the guild has ever known. And Felicia M. N. Sforza, among the few women ever accepted into our order but utterly indispensable all the same; knowing her way around more firearms and explosives than I may ever fully appreciate. Her uncanny knack of regularly crafting her own munitions that earned her the appropriate Company nickname of the *Alchemist*.

I was ever grateful to have them at my side for this fated mission. The last among us was a fresh recruit, Tommy McClain, a former gang runner from the Liver-chester cesspit of Oldham. Far too fresh for such a job normally, but the guild-masters felt his underworld knowledge would come in handy. Knowledge can prove a lifesaver, true, but only when your source of knowledge can stay on the damn raft long enough.

We were assigned upon the Forward Winds, a barge well known for transporting discreet shipments from third party investors. Alas their latest agreement involved the transportation of cargo of a highly sensitive and volatile nature. We were told nothing else, save that the contents was highly desired within the Birmingham wards and therefore must not be left visible to hungering eyes during the sunlit hours. Normally, a job of such dubious nature would fall outside the company's policy. However, the guild overseer had agreed to this assignment personally.

That final day before venturing into the black isles of the metropolis faded too soon. We camped a few miles from the city limits along the banks of the recently expanded Worchester canal. In spite of our dark thoughts, we had to keep a stoic air about us for Grigori, the Forward Wind's Squat and weary eyed captain; had to maintain the company reputation.

So we sat, huddled around the smoking remains of what we all suspected could well be our last meal, stealing glances at one another before turning our gazes back to the sea of soot visible just beyond the next grey hill. Over ten thousand factory chimneys painted the surrounding sky and lands with their foul pigments. The crisscrossing transit rails towered above miles of crumbling terrace lanes, industrial sectors, and slapdash markets. And cutting through it all were the canals, veining the whole city into hundreds of island holdings; literal territorial lines for the thousands of gangs, forever warring with one another for whatever smatterings of control they could seize within this *Venice of the North*.

One of my previous duties as a field commander had been to observe the battleground before making the charge. Overlooking the industrial metropolis, I mapped out our main journey whilst planning alternative routes, trusting my eyes and instincts to tell me which wards would prove to be our safest passage tonight, the worst parts fluctuating weekly. At the city's heart were the great glistening domes that housed the Gardens of Edgbaston, the University District and the Imperial Quarter, the latter of which was our destination upon the slopes of Colemore Heights. Once within those sanctuaries of the industrial elite, we would be safe. Supposedly.

...

With the sun vanishing over the horizon and setting the skies alight in evening fire, our barge began its steady course towards the thrice-damned metropolis. It's said that that even five miles from city's edge, the waters of Birmingham are toxic enough corrode flesh if left to soak long enough. Though it's never been a rumour I've felt any desire to test, I had to question validity of these claims as I watched scores of canal dwellers washing their rancid clothes at either side. Perhaps it was an exaggeration. Perhaps they're a hardier people with little other recourse.

The shacks adjoining both sides of the canal soon gave way to teetering wooden tenements as the sky slowly turned a billowing black and we crossed into the first ward of Redditch. Having only been recently assimilated into expanding behemoth that is Birmingham, the place still had the bearings of a country town and its citizens were still inclined to harken back to their routes, despite the many new factory chimneys we could spot all around us. Here at city's limits was safe as it were ever like to get within the unprotected wards, yet still I did not like the way that certain masked folk marked our barge's passing with hungry eyes.

We continued on our course, the air becoming more and more choked by the minute as additional tenements rose all around till they looked ready to collapse upon us, the sky growing blacker all the while, more from the clouds of factory smoke than the darkening night. Then, as we drove our way through the once green ward of Bournville our first would be boarders fell upon us.

A gunshot sounded from the cast iron railing to my left, ricocheting off the barge's port side. Immediately we all ducked down as further shots sounded from to the right. We looked desperately for signs of the attackers as we passed beneath a bridge. Tommy was the first to spot one from an upper balcony and brought the sharpshooter down in one shot. Perhaps the new recruit was worth more than I initially expected. Felicia held steady, her arsenal would have surely torn these amateurs to shreds but the collateral caused by them can be devastating.

Yet the attackers' efforts proved to be a feint as not even Algernon noticed the sleight figure atop the bridge until he dropped down and by that point it was too late. The boy was already pelting to the Forward Wind's edge clutching a small crate of cargo and made to leap for the near dockside but Algernon had by now whipped out a small hand pistol and fired it into the boy's spine. He cried out as his back blossomed crimson before toppling into the canal's depths taking the cargo with him.

I cursed under my breath and could sense that Felicia and Algernon had done likewise. We hadn't time to retrieve the fallen cargo. We had to keep going. Still, that lost asset would mean a considerable loss to our salary along with smearing the Company's name.

We pressed on with darkened resolves, retaliatory gunfire perusing our passing. So soon in our contract had we suffered a loss. One that, we knew, would not be our last, as we descended into the city's underbelly.

...

Heading ever closer to Birmingham's corporate heart, other canal ways branched off from ours with increasing regularity all the while our own byway widened as more vessels joined us on its course. As the city night came alive with sounds of drunken revelries, screaming loco-engines, and the cries of the destitute and dying, more eyes than we ever would have liked were on us and the suspicious unmarked cargo we were transporting.

We dared not break away from our current course to one of the branching byways as that would be as sure an act of suicide as any, being unfamiliar as we were with Birmingham's convoluted geography and with the many gangs that doubtlessly made business attacking ships foolish enough to detour into such arteries. We stayed on course; we had little choice now, come what may.

As our route widened further still, the city around expanded too. Soon titanic workhouses graced either side of the canal; towering like misshapen mausoleums of brick and mortar. I shudder to think of the horrors perpetrated in them day by day.

I hear the largest are owned by the city's greatest gangs, their unfortunate inhabitants numbering in the tens of thousands slaving over the manufacture of opioids and munitions alike, keeping a monopoly on the black market ever flowing. I've heard other tales too; tales about the all women workhouses becoming prison brothels by night for the youngest occupants. Tales that would doubtlessly make

113

Felicia take a Molotov to the Master's office right now if she believed it was happening in one of the very houses we passed.

Next we found ourselves passing some of the city's huge infirmaries, conveniently positioned next to the workhouses and to the central canal. With so many attacks, maladies, fires and industry accidents happening in the city on a regular basis; these "houses of care" were accosted by an overwhelming influx of the sick, injured and dying. So much so that special precautions had to be made to make way for new patients and that's what the hatches next to the canal were made for. Even as we passed I saw forms bound in yellowed cloth being deposited out of these slats and into the canal's black waters.

Smells clogged the night air; burning fuel, rotting skins, dysentery laced sewage and alcohol spiked piss and vomit congealing into a choking soup. I was not surprised to spy so many wayfarers concealing their mouths and noses in bound cloth. Not that it would avail them much. Brum's infamous stench can linger in the mouth and nostrils for days afterwards, and it never fully leaves your clothes so be sure not to dress in an outfit you're fond of when venturing here.

With the canal coming to its widest pass, as we headed steadily towards the juncture of the Five Ways where all major channels meet, we saw our ferries and barges drawing apart forming great dark expanses in the waters. A cool mist was already descending upon us but we knew that if we kept to wavering green lights of Pyr energy bathing the Imperial Quarter that we would stay on route.

Soon we could hardly see any boats near us and this struck me as quite unusual as the fog wasn't very thick. By the time we saw the dilapidated remains of barge loom out of night it was already too late. Knives cut into our raft's sides and the Cutters clambered on board.

They don't handle firearms, not the Cutters–as they've become known by those who brave Birmingham's Byways. Ammunition, after all, would become wet and useless in the canals. No, these bastards brandish knives, blades, spurs, shivs, glass shards, serrated hats, and practically anything else small and lethal on their persons. Protecting themselves from worst of the water's pollutants in rough pads and tanned hides with their eyes obscured behind tinted goggles, they lie in wait on the canal's shoreline or the wreckages of vessels already fallen to their predations before stealthily slipping into the waters and surrounding vulnerable drifters.

Their attacks were quick, brutal, and precise. Their victims are dead in less than a minute and that would doubtless have been the fate of our own venture had we not acted as speedily as we did.

Felicia was the first to open fire, the exploding shrapnel from her shot bursting the cutter's head apart into a fractured paste. Then the Forward Winds' navigator's gullet surrendered its life fluid to his Cutter captor who then threw the spasming wretch into the hungry murk below. With a quick shot from my rifle I let the Cutter join his quarry, but then crippling pain drove into my side as another of his ilk on my left bore down upon me.

I collapsed but my attacker followed suit as Tommy came to my rescue, smoke rising from his rifle as if time had slowed. I got back to my feet but pain still lanced up my left side, as the cutter's implement remained lodged there.

Cursing at my fortune, I looked upwards to see more of the fowl locusts launching themselves off the wrecked remains of the other barge. One of them never reached our deck as he lurched backwards from Algenon's shot and hit the water with the force of a small cannon blast. Tommy fired at the first to hit the deck striking them clean in the left calf. The last pelted straight for me and, had I not the training and experience to react against my crippling pain, I would doubtless not be recounting this encounter now.

I could see more Cutters lying in wait on the barge but Felicia had already let go their deaths: Her nitro sling-shot sailed majestically towards their barge before smacking the highest Cutter between the eyes. His face caved in for a split second and then his body exploded in alchemical fire releasing smaller pellets upon the former cutter's companions and the barge as a whole. Within three seconds of cracking devastation all that remained of the forsaken barge and its Cutter appropriates was flotsam and charred limbs.

Yet the fight was far from done. Gregori and his surviving crewmates had retreated into the Forward Winds' cabin and a Cutter had fallen upon Felicia. Pinning her to the ground, he attempted to slice her open with broken scissor fragments strapped to his knuckles. Yet the blades made only light gouges across her padded leather vest and the attacker quickly found himself missing the top half of his skull as Felicia's revolver sang. But before she could return to her feet another Cutter, a woman, judging by her physique, leapt down from the cabin above. Felicia only just had time to roll away before makeshift stilettoes drove into where she had been.

Algernon was currently engaged with another foe and I was pressed behind a crate, feverishly reloading my spent ammunition and so gestured to Tommy to go to Felicia's aid. She had already made a powerful kick at her assailant and sent them crashing into a crate causing its contents to spill forth. Glass phials of gently pulsing green gushed out. I saw Felicia's eyes widen. I saw the cutter struggle to steady herself with one of her blades and pierced one of the phials.

'Fucking–' was all Felicia could say before green light engulfed them both.

All sound was blotted out in that instant. Tommy was sent hurtling back from the sudden eruption on the Forward Wind's upper starboard side. The right side of the cabin was ripped asunder. The vessel lurched to one side. Crates of the cargo broke free from their binding and were sent cascading into the canal's depths or else crashing against their still secured kin, in one case crushing an awe struck Cutter. I clutched onto my crate with all the strength left in me, willing its restraints not to fail and, from the edge of my vision, I could see Algernon doing the same. My rifle had already vanished beneath the flickering water before I remembered to keep it secure.

When the initial chaos had run its course and I had become reacquainted with time, our fractured remains of a barge were hurtling off course and heading steadily towards the Five Ways Juncture. The few surviving Cutters already abandoned ship and it looked as though Algernon, Tommy and I were only occupants remaining.

The top right side of the vessel had been seemingly torn from this world with no trace of Felicia or her assailant remaining. Tommy lay sprawled against a crate screaming in agony. I staggered to his side, my left flank throbbing with every step, worried at what I would see. His right foot had been all but blasted away and his eyes were fussed shut as black tears seeped down his twisted countenance. A single surviving crewmember who had escaped the cabin just in time crawled over to us.

'God,' he breathed, 'just what-…'

'*Pyr*.' I said simply, fighting back the rage. 'Diluted *Pyr* energy cells.' So that had been the cargo. *Was* still the cargo. What was left of it at any rate. Though never my intent to speak ill of Company operations, I must confess that had we knowledge of such sensitive cargo we may well have been able to avert this catastrophe. May well have spared Felicia. A terrible loss of both a comrade in arms and a good woman. She'd joined the Company nearly fifteen years prior needing the funds necessary to support a fatherless household of five children by whatever means she could find; beginning with helping in the manufacture of Company patented munitions before the full breadth of her skills were discovered. An exemplary Company operative of whom you'll find many papers and journals within this very library. Never forget Felicia Maria Natalya Sforza for her talent may never again grace our guildhalls.

But I had little time to reflect on our fallen comrade for the remains of our barge were already beginning to tilt upwards and descend. More of our fateful cargo plunged into the canal's depths. Looking around desperately for a sign of the shore, I instead spied a small vessel that had fortuitously drifted close to us. A scavenger skiff by the look of its three occupants and lack of any cargo, likely come to see if there were any loot to take from our raft's remains.

Algernon exchanged a glance with me before tossing his hand-pistol. Catching it, I turned immediately to the skiff's occupants, indicating them to abandon ship. But they stood firm and gestured to their heaviest crewman who raised a shotgun to my head but a second later was sent toppling into the black waters by Algernon's lightning quick shot through one ear and out the other. The two survivors grudgingly threw up their hands and with another signal from me leapt overboard and began swimming to the nearest shore.

With not another moment to lose, Algernon began unstrapping the remaining cargo whilst I secured our new vessel. Biting back the pain in my side, I dragged Tommy's screaming wreck onto our vessel as our one surviving crewman, managing to regain his wits, began to assist Algernon. Within a minute we had transferred the few crates of cargo we had left and resigned the Forward Winds to its waterlogged tomb before carrying on towards the Five Ways.

...

I asked our surviving wayman, by the name of Frederick, who had hired us and why we weren't informed of the cargo's contents. He answered only that we were to transport the shipment down the New Hall pass to the Imperial Quarter. There, between 12 and 1AM, we were to meet our contractor. Grigori knew all the details, he said, and now the poor bastard had taken them to the grave with him.

Who in all hells would have contracted us to ship diluted *Pyr* energy cells? They are, after all, sole property of TITAN and they'd never need to hire an independent trading vessel when they owned transit lines to circulate their prize resource within hours. It was too much to think about at this time, in the middle of hostile territory with the prospect of a failed contract looming with ever increasing certainty over us. I'll say this now if you haven't already committed it to your soul: you only report a failed contract for the Company *once*. And trust me, the only way you'll want to fail the Company is to be killed on duty; it's honestly the better prospect than the alternative.

Duty kept us going if nothing else. Tommy's wails had receded to anguished sobs. Algernon was of the opinion that we be merciful to the young recruit rather than continue his suffering and threaten what remained of our assignment. I, however, believed that the boy was not yet done for: we live in an age of miracles, after all, where cripples can walk and the blind can yet see again. So instead we gagged him and prayed he would fall unconscious before long. I could only pray that my own injury would not worsen until after our task was complete.

Reaching the great conjunction of the Five Ways, we found a great clamour of vessels clustered around the gallows island at its centre. Even through the great wall of boats and rafts we could see the latest condemned lining the edge of the island, clouds of carrion fowl haloing their vigil. A futile farce by the authorities that some order still exists within the wards.

Eventually we saw the salvation from our hell as the great stone foundations of the Imperial dome steadily rose before us, silhouettes of majestic towers visible just beyond its glassy circumference. A little to the left of the great central tunnel into the quarter, where catastrophic custom checks most certainly awaited us, the smaller disused New Hall tunnel marked the entryway to our destination. We passed beneath and found soon found ourselves navigating a murky abyss. All visible light reduced to the lamp at our skiff's prow.

Since entering, Tommy had quieted down. So I tenderly removed his gag and he began to mutter. Quietly, admittedly, but the tunnel magnified his babbling. He raved of Green light in his eyes, Green light that was trapped there, would never leave him, never give him rest, forever burning his vision. It began making us sick so I placed the gag back on him.

My side burned from the cutter's blade but I knew I couldn't pull it out. Not here, when we were still so exposed and had only the most basic binding on us. We had to finish this mission first and we were so close. So instead I focussed my mind on a face I only saw in my dreams now. A face whom I knew from my time during the Persian revolts and whom I shared a love that was as true as it was forbidden.

...

A light began to shimmer in the darkness ahead. Shining on bricks. A turn in the tunnel. The light increased as we approached the turn, then we were bathed in blaring torchlight as what looked to be at least a score awaited us at the gate to the port. Men and women in pinstriped shirts and rough spun waist jackets perched on crates and barrels at either side of the closed metal gates. Each was wielding a firearm and one

119

manically smiling gang runner leered above us aiming a Gatling gun.

'Took you fucking long enough.' Said a voice from behind the band. Looking up we saw a woman of such delicateness and beauty that she seemed almost unnatural to look upon. There was an oriental look to her. Skin like porcelain. Even with the thick Brum accent her voice possessed a certain unearthly tone that had nothing to do with the echo of these tunnels.

'And who do you presume we are?' Said Algernon.

'My fucking delivery boys,' she descended from her perch and moved towards, 'at least I fucking hope you are 'cause you don't anything like I asked for. I requested a barge of cargo fully crewed, a group of Company men for protection and instead I get one boatman, two company men, plus one who looks to be on death's door, and about a fourth of what I paid for.'

'Do you expect us to believe you're the one who hired the Company?' said Algernon incredulously, 'We have a reputation to maintain and would never think to barter with—' but I gave him a knowing look and he quickly trailed off. No, this individual had just confirmed what I had been speculating ever since the nature of our cargo had been revealed. Who else would have asked for *Pyr* cells to be delivered in secret under cover of night? The Company has a reputation true, and it has secrets that we're all sworn to keep. What I'm revealing to you now is just the tip of the confidences you'll be sworn to during your time with us.

'I hope you know what you're getting into,' I told the gang's leader apparent, 'if TITAN gets wind of the munitions you've acquired...'

'They won't, and you're *noble* Company name won't be implicated, you have my word. Part of the condition of hiring you.' She looked disdainfully down at us. 'Can't say I'm too pleased with your performance. What happened to the Forward Winds and rest of my cargo?'

'Cutter attack on the Sparkbrook Grand Canal.' And I explained the events leading to the loss of barge and much of the Cargo.

'Fucking carelessness is what I call it. I hired you for top service and you lost over half my shipment. A near fucking disaster might be more accurate. We'll take what's left and what's due to us.' She nodded to an assistant to her left who raised a revolver towards our skiff. 'One of you already paid with their lives for that cockup but I'm gonna need another for that loss. Your boy looks like he's just begging for death so seems fair.'

'Tommy is still a Company man.' I bellowed back at her, 'slay him and there'll be recompense.'

'*Fuck*, your Light Brigade policies really are a pain in the arse.' She shrugged and nodded to her executioner. Seconds later Frederick was sent crashing into the waters behind us. A gaping maw in his forehead.

...

The following morning at first light, Algernon and myself were seated in a transit loco compartment, soaring above Birmingham's industrial isles. The urban wastelands seemed to stretch on and on until we were finally away and returning to Londinium. My left torso had been stitched and dressed up. Tommy was taken into intensive care back in the capital where I was told he later succumbed to his injuries. An infection in the stump of his right leg was the official cause yet I suspect something far darker. Of course TITAN would never want the inherent dangers of over-exposure to their "salvation" resource becoming public knowledge. Perhaps his death was a mercy in the end. One that I should have granted sooner. I still remember his gibberings of agonised terror as he was taken away.

If you take anything from this recount of mine then I hope it is this: be prepared for anything when venturing into Birmingham, which is a nigh-on impossible task but one that is essential to surviving nevertheless. Think fast and improvise because by God is that what the denizens of those wards do on a daily basis. The gangs are clever, making new adaptations to hijacking cargo with each passing year so you need to adapt with them.

Don't concern yourself overly with the nature of our client in this venture, whose name I later found out was Caroline Shen. Another lesson about our Company too but one

121

you will doubtless discover soon enough anyway. Incidentally, I have heard nothing of Ms Shen since, meaning she either lived up to her words and has kept a discreet profile or TITAN have done a successful job at wiping her and the gang she controls utterly from all heresay. Regardless, the Company have clearly not been implicated as has always been the case.

And here lies the final lesson to take from this. In spite of all complications, be they from rival arms for hire, corporate institutions, criminal cells, the monolith that is TITAN or even dissent from their own ranks: The Company Endures.

Captain Randal Harling Vanderman 47th Captain of the Light Brigade Company.

ABOUT THE AUTHORS

NICHOLAS DORAN was born in South Birmingham and has always been intrigued by the creation of imaginary worlds and the ways in which they inspire creativity in others. He specializes in dark and quirky speculative fiction and has previously had two short stories published in *Lifelines: an Anthology 2016*. When he is not writing, he often pursuing his second greatest passion in tabletop roleplaying. You can find out more about him and follow his blog on: **nicholasjdoran.uk**

ALISTAIR MATTHEWS is a lifelong Brummie and frequenter of public houses he is chuffed to contribute this tale. His only previous experience of seeing myself in print is a piece for a local parish magazine. His boss asked him to write something celebrating the centenary of the building they worked in. He enjoyed doing the research and the writing. His boss and the vicar were pleased anyway!

STEFFAN JONES is a Welsh-Irish Careers adviser and psychology graduate who grew up in rural south wales and had lived in several UK cities. He writes longer historical fiction and some experimental shorter things around politics, dating and adult entertainment world like escorts, brothels, strip clubs etc. This is his first published writing.

JULIE SPICER grew up in the West Midlands of England, where she still lives. An avid and enthusiastic reader from childhood she now indulges her passion for writing and is the author of the Edward Gamble Mystery novels (*The Art of Detection, Canvassing Crime* and *The Mystery Artist*), and of the Blackbridge crime series (*Fallout* and *Sweet Murder*).

DAVID CROSER grew up in the far north of England, in the Border country. As well as editing this anthology he is the author of *Rice Pudding Reality*, an anthology of his early short stories, *Four Seasons of Foche*, featuring his psychic French detective Eric Foche. He has also contributes stories to a number of other anthologies, *The Terror Tree Pun Book of Horror, Cadavers, Worlds of The Unknown 2* and *Worlds of the unknown 4*. His latest anthology, *A Foretaste of Infinity*, is published in January. He lives in Solihull with his hubbie and three cats.

BERNI SORGA-MILLWOOD works as a primary school teacher in Birmingham. She taught in schools across London for many years before joining VSO (Voluntary Services Overseas). As a VSO volunteer, she worked in the Solomon Islands for a number of years training teachers and running workshops. After returning to London, she took some writing courses at Goldsmith College and The City Lit. She has written a number of short stories, books for children and a novel inspired by her time spent in the Solomon Islands. She is currently working on her second novel.

CHRISTOPHER P. GARGHAN was born and raised in Birmingham and is the current Chair of Birmingham Writers' Group. The city of a thousand trades winds itself into his every story, no matter the genre. Christopher is currently seeking a publisher for his debut novel, *The Boat People.*

RICHARD PRESTON has only been with the Birmingham Writer's Group for the better part of a year, but he has already managed to make a name for himself by winning their Summer Short Story Competition. He also used to work at BM&AG, hence the inspiration for this story. This is his first published story, short or otherwise, but he writes non-fiction of a decidedly nerdy nature
at **www.fnordcolourcomics.wordpress.com**

MATT JOINER has sometimes in their career in Birmingham Writers' Group called on them to become a secret historian of Birmingham and talking tapeworm! Their stories and poems have been published in the likes of *Not One of Us, Lackington's* and *Sein Und Werden* (where 'The Mummers' Boy' first appeared). They enjoy real ale, photosynthesis and flippancy.